JED and the Junkyard Rebellion

STEVEN BOHLS

DISNEP • HYPERION

LOS ANGELES   NEW YORK

for Jackie

First Edition, February 2019
1 3 5 7 9 10 8 6 4 2
FAC-020093-19004
Printed in the United States of America
This book is set in Adobe Caslon Pro Fontspring
Designed by Maria Elias and Phil Buchanan

Library of Congress Cataloging-in-Publication Data
Names: Bohls, Steven, author.
Title: Jed and the junkyard rebellion / Steven Bohls.
Description: First edition. • Los Angeles ; New York : Disney Hyperion,
2019. • Summary: Jed's potential is unlocked, but even more questions
arise as he confronts his past and contemplates his future.
Identifiers: LCCN 2018052239 • ISBN 9781484730485 (hardcover : alk. paper)
Subjects: • CYAC: Science fiction. • Automata—Fiction. • Heroes—Fiction.
Classification: LCC PZ7.1.B645 Jc 2019 • DDC [Fic]—dc23
LC record available at https://lccn.loc.gov/2018052239

Reinforced binding

Visit www.DisneyBooks.com

Prologue

The Jenkins Home

At well past four in the morning after her son's twelfth birthday, Mary Jenkins sat with Jed and her husband on the end of their bed. Jed's eyes drooped, and his head tipped forward. "He's nodding off," she whispered to Ryan.

Jed's head snapped upright. "Nope. I'm completely awake," he said. But a yawn betrayed him.

Mary smiled and kissed his forehead. "Go to bed." He wiped the smudge of red lipstick with the back of his arm. She knew he hated it, but that's just how boys his age were. And moms were supposed to kiss them anyway. "Did you have a good birthday?"

Jed smiled back. "The best."

"How does it feel to be twelve?" Ryan asked. "Any different?"

Jed shrugged. "Not as much as I thought."

"That's the way with things," Ryan said. "They don't often happen how we picture them." He hopped off the bed and extended a hand to Mary. "Madame, might I have the pleasure of your company in the kitchen for a bit of late-night dish washing?"

"Certainly, my prince." Mary took Ryan's hand and leaped into his arms.

He stumbled with the unexpected pounce. "To the kitchen!" he said, his hand high as if holding a sword.

"I can help," Jed said, eyes bleary.

"If you'd like," Ryan said. "But there's to be a fair bit of kissing, romantic dancing, and more kissing."

"Good night," Jed said.

"See you in the morning, honey," Mary called.

They began tidying up, but before they'd cleared even an armful of dishes, Ryan doused his fingers under the running tap and splashed Mary with water.

She giggled, trying to dodge a second splash.

"You won't escape," Ryan said, dipping his hand under the tap water again.

"Shh," Mary whispered. "You'll wake him."

Ryan's head shifted to look at Jed's bedroom, and Mary dunked her whole hand into a cup of water and swatted it at him. Water sprayed over his face. He gave an exaggerated look of shock. "Trickery!"

She flicked more water at him. "Always."

Mischief filled Ryan's face.

Mary shrieked and fled the kitchen.

He chased.

But Mary was fast—she had always been faster than Ryan. She ran to the study and Ryan followed.

Safely inside, she tried to shut the door, but Ryan blocked the gap with a gangly, outstretched arm.

"Trapped," he said, grinning.

He slowly pushed the door open. Mary giggled again, backing away.

Ryan inched forward like a lion closing in on its cornered prey.

And then a soft sound shattered everything.

The cat-and-mouse chase.

The sneaky smiles.

The laughter in their eyes.

The joy in the air.

Chik, ch-chik, ch-chik, ch-chik, ch-chik.

Mary's heart wrenched.

No. Not now. Not after all this time.

They turned to the old typewriter in the corner bureau and listened to the *ch-chik, ch-chik* of its yellowed keys as they pressed down on their own. One at a time. Printing letters on a page that hadn't felt new ink in many years.

Ryan held Mary close as they stepped toward the typewriter. The keys punched faster, black letters stamping the paper.

Ching!

The machine rang out and the barrel swung on its own to begin another line. They hovered over the typewriter, reading the letter as it typed.

Javelin Agents 394 and 395,

GOLDEN KING has emerged from the fog with another autonomous relic (designation: GILDED RELIC BETA).

AGENT 1121 boarded the RED GALLEON and has retrieved the relic. GOLDEN KING is in pursuit. Copper gearsmiths have discovered GILDED RELIC BETA was engineered for the purpose of finding and recovering GILDED RELIC ALPHA—still presently in your possession.

Operation LOOSE PIGEON has been reopened.

Return immediately through the FRINGE and meet us twelve sunfalls east of BASE 11-14-1 where you will assume guardianship over GOLDEN RELIC BETA until gearsmiths can further analyze her purpose.

All speed,
Captain J. Butterfly
Authentication code: WHISPERS OVER THE WALL

Mary read the words. She read them again. And again.

"We can't go," she said.

Ryan folded the letter and put it into his pocket. "We have to. Now."

"But—" Mary looked over her shoulder toward Jed's room. "He's—"

Ryan gripped Mary's shoulders. "If Lyle finds him, he'll no longer be our Jed. I won't let that happen. We have the two quickest wasps in the fleet. We'll meet with Butterfly, pick up the girl, and be back before Jed wakes up. This will be over before you know it. Okay?"

Mary nodded. "Okay."

"I'll pack the typewriter and gather supplies. Leave the key on the table, just in case, and get the shatterdrill."

Mary hurried to the kitchen and opened a hidden panel in the pantry behind the green beans. There, untouched for so long, was the key. Jed's key.

She pressed her lips to its aged metal. "Be safe, my Jed."

"Ready?" Ryan asked.

She nodded.

They set the key on the table, opened the dishwasher, and entered the tunnel to the fringe.

Time had treated the tunnel well. The shatterdrill-melted path was still a cavern of solid metal. Their wasps were at the tunnel exit where they'd left them. The ships were so much smaller than Mary remembered. It was all these years of driving in cars at least four times the size of the small yellow airships. She climbed inside and dusted off the control panel.

"Light the way," Ryan called, sliding into his own wasp.

Mary lifted the shatterdrill. It had been so long since she'd used the relic. She aimed it at the end of the tunnel, which had grown cluttered from years of junkstorms. Light blasted from the shatterdrill's tip and carved a fresh path in the junk.

Ryan's wasp hummed as its engines flared. He gave her a wink and then yanked the accelerator. His ship shot forward so fast that she didn't have time to wink back.

"Okay, girl," she whispered to her own wasp, "you and I are good friends, remember? Help me keep Jed safe, all right?" She gripped the accelerator. "Let's go."

She pulled, and her body pinned itself to the back of her seat. The speed was astonishing—impossible even. Her wasp shot from the tunnel. She looked around at the sun-glittered metal below. "Welcome home."

They found Butterfly's steamboat in less than two hours—nearly an hour after the dread had arrived. Black masses polluted the sky with their twisted shapes and smoke that hung like oil in the air. Rockets whistled past them. Orange bursts of light rained fire and acid.

In a breath, Mary's mind transformed. She was no longer a homeowner association's vice president. She was a javelin. Her hands whipped over the controls. The tiny wasp launched stingers at dread warships. The stingers pulsed and detonated, breaking ships in two and sending giant chunks of debris raining down on the junk fields below.

The battle raged while she and Ryan cut through the fray to reach a landing dock in the steamboat.

Captain Butterfly met them at the bay doors.

Mary opened the wasp's hatch. "Butterfly!"

"Mary, Ryan."

"Where is she?" Ryan asked. "Where's the girl?"

"It's gone," Butterfly said. "Escaped. We have to find it. Now."

The steamboat shook with a heavy impact and then began to descend in slow motion.

"We're going down, Captain," someone yelled.

The ship tilted; the wasps slid across the docking bay. Ryan and Mary ran after the small ships, but a barrage of fire shook the steamboat and knocked them off-balance.

"In here." Ryan grabbed Mary's arm.

He pulled her into a storage closet.

The steamboat hit the junkyard floor.

Mary tried to think—to listen—to speak. But everything felt fuzzy.

Something struck her hard in the back of the head, and her vision went black.

. . .

When Mary awoke, the sounds of battle were gone. No gunfire. No shouting. The ship was still. Silent. The only noise that filled the space was faint clicks, like beetles being crushed under a shoe. Everything was dark. She was still inside the storage closet, but Ryan was gone. And there was something in her hand.

It was a piece of paper, folded and tucked into her palm. She felt around for the closet door handle and quietly twisted it open. Light leaked into the small space. It was just enough for her to make out Ryan's handwriting.

Mary,

The Red Galleon is here with Lyle. He got Butterfly. I'm so sorry. Lyle took Butterfly's appearance to set a trap for Jed. I'm going to the Red Galleon.

Copper Headquarters is watching the tunnel exit for Jed.

Go to Lawnmower Mountain. Get there before Lyle. He's making his move. Hurry.

Ryan

"Go to Lawnmower Mountain . . . ?" she whispered. They weren't supposed to contact them unless it was absolutely necessary. If Lyle were here, she could be followed—she could lead him straight there.

But she trusted Ryan, and if he said she needed to fly to Lawnmower Mountain, then that's what she'd do.

She stayed hidden until the sounds of crushing beetles stopped. When it was quiet, she left the closet and walked to the main deck. A small footstep crunched on debris behind her. She turned cautiously toward the sound.

A girl about Jed's age—her head cocked—watched Mary with curiosity. She was small . . . thin . . . with hair like a spool of copper.

"Hello," Mary said. "What's your name?"

"Shay. What's yours, little *mouse?*"

"It's Mary."

Shay shook her head. "No, it's not. It's wicked little *Scritcherling!*"

"No—no, I'm not one of them. I promise."

"Not yet." Shay cocked her head the other way. "I'll fix that. Come here, little mouse."

Mary ran, and Shay bounded after her.

"You're a scampery little mouse, aren't you?" Shay called.

Shay ran faster, gaining on Mary. When Shay was only a few steps away, Mary stopped dead, spun around, and kicked her heel into the air. It collided with Shay's face, and she flipped onto her back.

When she rose, she cocked her head again. The wickedness in her eyes was gone.

"Where am I?" She looked around and shrank against a wall. "This place feels like 'alone.'"

Mary backed away slowly.

Shay shook her head. "No," she said. "Mouse king told me to make scritches. Lots and lots of scritches. I'm supposed to make scritches." She looked up at Mary. "Am I supposed to make scritches?"

Mary shook her head. "Mouse king told me you were done. You can go home now."

Shay thought for a moment, and then her eyes narrowed. "Home? I don't have a home! You're a lying mouse! I know when little mice lie."

Mary bolted for the wasp. Ten steps . . . five . . . two . . . She leaped into the air and slid feetfirst into the cockpit.

Engines roared as she yanked the accelerator. Flames from the boosters shot backward into Shay, setting bits of her shirt on fire.

The wasp wobbled as it lifted from the cargo bay and into the open air. A tugboat—a *dread* tugboat—approached the steamboat, moving directly toward her.

"Let's go," Mary said. "Get me out of here."

The tugboat readied its shatterkegs.

"Go, go, go!" she said.

The engines crackled. The wasp shot away. The tugboat disappeared behind her.

"Good girl," she said, patting her wasp's dashboard. "Let's get to Lawnmower Mountain."

She reached for the throttle and then hesitated. Dark clouds billowed up ahead. *No . . . not clouds. Dreadnoughts.*

Mary turned to the right, but three battlenoughts hovered in place. To the left was a pack of ghostnoughts. She was surrounded.

"Come on, baby," she whispered. "Let's figure a way out of this."

Orange specs flowered from the ships around her. The sound of the shatterfire followed. Mary yanked the controls and the wasp shot to the side. Left, then right, then left again, she dodged a barrage of shells. She was a dancer twirling through the sky. No one flew like a copper javelin—and no copper javelin flew like Mary or Ryan.

Squads of ships launched a storm of shatterfire; Mary nimbly evaded them all.

Until something hard struck her left engine.

A whistling screeched from the wasp, followed by a loud popping. Mary could barely fly through the shatterfire with both engines; there was no hope with just one. A shell smashed into one of her wings. The wasp caught fire and the engines wailed.

"Land," she told herself. "You need to land."

Decisively, Mary began to descend. Just then, a shell pierced the windshield, and her wasp exploded.

Jed

Jed lifted a dented shaft of metal to his chest and slid it into the golden keyhole.

A click echoed in his ears.

The golden panel just above the keyhole popped open.

Under the panel was a large red button.

He reached for the button and pressed it.

Something inside him awakened. It was small and bright . . . a piece of him that had slept for many years. And now, after all this time, it began to glow. He couldn't immediately see a difference in his skin or the exposed gears in his chest, but he could sense it. As the glowing feeling intensified, a dull light shone through the keyhole. Shay and Jed's father stared intently at the light.

"What's happening to me?" Jed asked.

"Guardian Mouse," Shay whispered.

Jed's dad looked at her and then to Jed. He opened his mouth as if to explain, but before he could, the heat in Jed's chest flared. His frame hummed. An electric charge coursed through his bones. The energy burned hotter. A stinging, blistering fire blazed through his blood.

And then every bit of heat from every corner of his body contracted into an inferno in his chest. Jed fell to his knees, clutching his heart.

His vision rattled. A buzz cut into his ears. The pain, the heat, and the sound collided, firing a pulse of energy that shook the barge with a deafening crack. A ring of light blasted from his chest. The light swelled across the horizon and then disappeared behind the fog that walled them in.

Jed's world went silent.

An icy chill bit at his chest that no longer held the raging sun.

Darkness crept into the edges of his vision. Then everything vanished. The barge. His father. Shay. All of them—*gone.*

. . .

A sea of blackness swirled into focus as the color drained from the world.

The air smelled like oil and tasted like metal. Smokey tendrils hovered like fog—scratchy, dusty particles that felt like slivers of glass.

Where am I . . . ?

Everything ached. His joints . . . hands . . . neck . . . even his eyes. The pain came in waves, pulsing from head to knee in steady, angry surges. He felt as if he'd been asleep for a solid month.

Slowly, the blackness sharpened into clarity, and the throbbing pain quieted.

Where . . . where am I . . . ?

He lifted his arm and held it in front of his face. The hand before his eyes was unfamiliar. He tried to move the curious fingers. They wiggled. But this wasn't how he remembered his fingers. They had been different. Shinier. Like *gold*. But these . . . these fingers looked more like hot dogs.

"So squishy . . ." he whispered, clenching and unclenching his fingers into a fist.

Even the sound of his own voice was peculiar . . . foreign . . . *fake*.

Who am I?

He tried to think. The image of a burning heat melting his mind surfaced. He shook his head. Memories felt buried and looked blurry—dreams he could not remember.

What am I?

I have a name . . . don't I?

He tried to remember—*anything*. His home? His face? The harder he tried, the soupier his brain felt.

He searched the darkness. He was in a cave. No . . . not a cave. An empty water tower on its side. Wooden windmill blades obscured the entrance. Through the gaps, he saw bits of the outside world. The ground was compressed junk. The sky was a dusty black expanse.

Near the entrance of the water tower sat a raft, quiet and still. He stared at it. A vibrant green tree with bright yellow lemons sprouted from its center.

"Odd. Boats don't grow trees . . . *do they*?" Jed whispered to himself.

This was all wrong. This wasn't where he belonged. Was it?

He didn't live under dark mist that tasted like oil and metal. He lived in a three-bedroom home, with color and smiles. Didn't he?

He twisted his neck. To his left was a sleeping girl—her small body curled into a ball. She had copper hair that glinted in the dim sliver of light, and her tiny mouth sipped quick breaths of air. She shivered and pulled her legs closer to her chest. Then she sighed and twitched her nose.

To his right was a sleeping man, tall, gangly, and sprawled out sloppily. He drew slow, heavy breaths and released low—almost silent—snores.

Who are they?

"They're dangerous . . ." a voice whispered in his ear.

Jed's heart thumped at the sound. It wasn't his own voice. It was a man's. Someone he knew.

"Who . . . are you?" he whispered back.

"A friend," said the whisper. "And I'm going to help you escape."

"Escape from what?"

"From those two. They stole you. They are thieves. Get away from them. Hurry!"

"I don't remember you. I don't . . . I don't remember anything."

"I know," the voice whispered. "I'll help you remember. Now, crawl away."

The gangly man beside him rolled onto his side and snorted.

"What's going on?" Jed whispered. "This isn't right. I'm not supposed to be here."

A thought floated into his mind of warm beds . . . warm carpets . . . birthdays and laughter. There was no laughter here. Only darkness and strangers.

The whisper returned. "The connection is fading. You must find me. Look for the red flares. Go. Quickly!"

Icy needles prickled up Jed's spine. Fear welled in his chest, and his thoughts shattered in a frenzy of panic.

Run.

Get away.

Hide.

Carefully, he crept out of the water tower and into the darkness.

Jed

Ships hung heavy in the sky like storm clouds. *Dreadnoughts.* Jed knew the word, he knew he'd seen them before, and he knew they were deadly. He scanned the horizon for a clue. A flickering red light streamed through the sky. *Look for the red flares*, the voice had said.

"Are you there?" Jed closed his eyes and searched for the whisper. His mind was a vault of locked memories. The whisper was the key, he imagined. He was in a strange place with strange people. *I was taken? By them?*

He moved from cover to cover, toward the flare. Above, the dreadnoughts flew in jumbled fleets. The ship hulls were twisted hunks of metal. An eerie jaggedness framed the bodies of the beasts, and orange furnaces burned in the heart of each ship, leaking a dull glow.

As Jed watched, a distant fleet began to change course, turning until they were pointed directly at him.

They can't see me from that far away . . . can they?

Their engines flared, making the air ripple with heat and bringing the dreadnoughts closer.

Jed's heart thumped. He stumbled away as the ships powered through the sky.

Up ahead, another fleet turned and faced him. They, too, began to accelerate.

"You've got to be kidding me," Jed said.

Faster and faster he ran, avoiding deadly misstep after deadly misstep on the uneven terrain. The ships were gaining on him. Jed shifted direction and sprinted left, away from both fleets. The ships maintained a steady course, and that's when he realized—the ships weren't heading for him. They were heading for each other.

BOOM! BOOM! BOOM!

Orange fire shot into the air and junk rumbled under Jed's feet. He followed the shatterfire with his eyes as it arced through the sky. Flames trailed the blasts as they slammed into one another, and explosions erupted from the broken hulls.

Jed ducked behind a tire as metal rained down and impaled the ground around him. The fleets continued firing and more metal slashed through the debris. Watching the destruction, Jed sensed a problem. The battle was off-kilter; it was strange . . . it was wrong. Why were the dreadnoughts firing at *each other*?

More scrap pelted the ground nearby, embedding itself in a fridge and leaving jagged metal chunks shivering upright in the junk. He swallowed nervously. The shatterkegs rumbled above him. "I need to get out or I'll be buried here."

Something cracked over Jed's head. Engines sputtered and wailed from one of the dreadnoughts. The storm paused, almost as if the enemies were taking a deep breath. Jed peeked out to see a dreadnought slowly being torn in half.

And then it began falling.

He leaped from behind the tire and sprinted away. He stole quick glances upward as both halves of the dreadnought sunk toward the ground. Jed's feet hit the junk faster and harder as a shadow swelled around him and the dreadnought fell closer. The nose of the ship pierced the ground first, metal shrieking in protest and debris shooting into the sky. Jed watched as the rest of the ship plummeted down.

"Go, go, go!" he yelled to himself.

Everything shook.

His lungs burned, but Jed kept running. Junk ripped, screeched, creaked, and shattered around him as smoke billowed up from the broken vessel. Figures emerged from the smoke. Black dots poked out and skittered in all directions. Before long, they swarmed the deck and crawled to the ground. They were twisted, misshapen scraps of flesh and metal.

Dread. The word lurked in the corner of Jed's empty mind just like *dreadnought* had.

He stumbled backward.

Dread from both sides met in the center of the battlefield, giving Jed a sliver of a chance to escape. He backed away until he thought it was safe, and then he ran until he could no longer hear the sounds of tearing metal. Distant ships flew in clusters toward other fleets. Dots of orange shatterfire speckled the dark sky. This was war. *But it isn't right. Why are the dread killing one another? They aren't supposed to do that. They're supposed to kill humans . . . meat sacks . . . aren't they?*

Jed dropped down behind a grimy couch to catch his breath, and the unfamiliar—yet familiar—whisper returned. "Traitors . . ."

"What?"

"I gave them life, and they turned into feral dogs."

Jed stared at the distant warring dread. "You created those things? Why?"

There was a long pause. "To survive." Another faint red flare shot up in the distance. "Quickly," the voice said. "Before they find you."

"Who?" Jed asked. "The dread?" But he could feel that the whisper was already gone.

The desolation was endless, mirroring the dark hole his questions had dug within him. Where was he? What was this place—this strange land of charred, squished-up junk and metal creatures?

A thought pricked the back of his mind: *This isn't land at all. It's a giant ship. A barge.*

He shook his head. That was ridiculous. A *ship?* The

horizon on all sides of him ended in a distant gray fog. This couldn't be a ship. That was impossible. It was too enormous; ships this big didn't exist. But, even as he tried to shake the thought from his mind, something told him that this was, indeed, a ship.

He looked up. Ships were flying above him, blasting each other to scrap. How could he be *standing* on one? It didn't make sense.

Why couldn't he remember? What was wrong with him? He stared at his hands again. *Who am I?* The skin was too soft and too pink. It didn't look right. Wasn't his skin . . . *gold?* He flexed his fingers one by one. "Who am I?" he said again, this time out loud. "I have a name. I know I do. My name is—" he spoke, as if the answer would somehow spring free on its own by doing so.

It didn't.

"My name is—" he tried again.

Nothing.

A dull ache throbbed in the center of his chest. Carefully, he pulled off his T-shirt. A long white bandage had been wrapped around his chest, and red oil seeped through the gauze. He unpinned the two aluminum clasps holding the wrap in place and let it unravel. When it reached its end, the fabric tugged against the dried red. He winced, pulling it off.

A ring of skin had burned away, revealing the delicate gears that spun inside his chest. *Golden* gears.

Panic ignited in the pit of his stomach. The gears inside him whirred faster as the terror clawed through his mind.

"*What* . . . what am I?" he whispered. "What's happening to me?"

His heartbeat quickened even more, and so did the golden gears. They hummed so silently that he might have never noticed them. The machinery spun around a golden plate with a keyhole in it. Jed ran his shaking fingers over the indentation.

Taking a deep breath, Jed leaned back against an old trunk and stared up at the sky, dropping his hands. He couldn't think about everything so much. He didn't want to. He had to worry about one thing at a time, and there were plenty of things to choose from.

The fog gave no indication whether it was morning, afternoon, or the middle of the night. Jed's stomach grumbled. Whatever time it was, he was hungry.

What did people eat here? *People?* He laughed at the word. Whatever those things crawling from the dreadnought were, they weren't *people*.

But they were at least partially alive, so that meant they had to eat *something*.

Jed stood and searched the ground around him.

A checkered pillow . . . a ladder . . . a painting of a dolphin.

The longer he walked, the more his stomach grumbled. But amidst doorknobs, stuffed bears, and a weed whacker, he couldn't spot anything to eat. What if there wasn't any food at all around here? What if the dread didn't *actually* eat food and instead ate *junk?* Jed touched the burned hole in his chest. Did *he* eat junk?

It had been hours since he'd seen a dread. Every so often,

another red flare would launch into the sky. He was getting closer, little by little.

His stomach rumbled again.

Just as he decided that there was no food in this wasteland, his tired eyes spotted a torn label with a muscly, green-skinned man standing in a meadow. Green Giant French Style Green Beans.

Jed grabbed the can. "Of course," he mumbled, "I'm in a world of junk with a can of green beans and no can opener."

He searched until he found a screwdriver to pry open the lid. He pounded and pulled until at last, he pinched one of the squishy green beans. The moment it touched his tongue, a memory popped open. Crisp green beans, pan-seared in olive oil and rolled in a bed of minced sautéed garlic cloves . . . hot turkey that steamed on a chrome platter . . . buttered broccoli, yams, and cranberry sauce. He was back home, sitting at the kitchen table for a Thanksgiving meal. As he chewed the cold, wet canned green beans, part of him wished the memory hadn't returned. It hung there, taunting him with safety and comfort.

He tipped the can to his chin and slurped the last few drops of water. Jed closed his eyes and thought of his warm home and warm meals once more. It was filled with shadows, but the outlines were there. Then, a new scratchy voice entered his mind.

"Wake up, Sleepy Mouse."

Jed's vision flickered. He sat still, focusing on the image. He was seeing double—a second sight overlaid on his own. He was looking through two sets of eyes at the same time.

"Wake up, Sleepy Mouse . . . wake up," the voice said again.

The vision saturated his sight until it was all he could see. Even with his eyes closed, the second pair of eyes revealed a new world to him. The voice grew louder. And then, all at once, everything that he was disappeared. Jed was in another mind.

Shay

"Wake up, Sleepy Mouse, wake up." Shay shook Ryan's shoulders with both hands. He flopped and wiggled more like a stepped-on mouse than an alive mouse. "Wake *up!*" she squeaked, pulling extra yankingly.

"Wh-what's going on?" Ryan asked, groggy from sleep.

Shay folded her arms and showed him her serious eyes. "Broken Mouse scampered away. *That's* what's going on."

"Broken . . . *huh?*" In half a squeak, Ryan's eyes widened in panic. "What happened? Where did he go? He's gone!"

Shay didn't unfold her arms and didn't stop showing him her serious eyes. "That's what I've been trying to say while you were pretending to be a stepped-on mouse."

"Where is he?"

She smooshed her finger to his lips. "Hush. Unless you want a scritcherling nest to hear you."

He nodded, but his eyes were still panicky.

"What did you see?" he squeaked, quieter this time.

"Hmm . . . well . . . I was having a dream about golden skies and blue puddles—puddles so *big* that little mouselings need little boats to cross them. I was on a yellow boat. It had yellow doors and yellow floors and green doorknobs. And then I woke up."

"And then what?"

"And then I woke *you* up. And then you asked me what happened. And then I told you that I was having a dream about golden skies and blue puddles—puddles so *big* that little mouselings—"

"You didn't see where he went?"

Shay scrunched her brow. "I already told you what I saw, and then I told you again. This isn't a time to be a forgetful mouse. It's a time to be a thinking mouse."

"We have to find him." Ryan cupped his hands to his mouth, about to shout.

"Hush!" This time Shay covered his mouth with *all* her fingers. "Do you want scritchmites to find Broken Mouse and break him even more?"

Ryan shook his head like an obedient mouseling.

She nodded. "Good. Then help me search the ground for Broken Mouse scamperings."

Ryan and Shay searched for a trail leading to Broken Mouse—for some sign of his whereabouts or movements. Ryan's face grew more and more wrinkly.

Suddenly, a sharp whistle sounded overhead. Shatterfire burst across the sky, soaring from one dreadnought to another. Explosions crackled between the two ships.

Ryan ducked as a hunk of metal crashed to the ground. "I don't understand," he said, tight frustration in his tone. "Why are they killing one another? We've been stuck hiding here for nearly three weeks waiting for the dread fighting to end, but it's just getting worse."

"My guess? Hmm . . . I'd bet a basketful of cheese that mouse king isn't mouse king anymore," Shay said.

"And so suddenly all the dread in the armada want to kill one another?"

"Little scritchbugs squeak and nibble at one another's tails, all trying to be new mouse king. But new mouse king is coming. . . ." she said. "I can smell it. Can't you smell it? It smells like sneakery. And pineapple."

"Huh?"

"It's a pokey fruit," she said. "Yellow and shiny. Tangy and sweet. Prickly and juicy. Squishy and—"

"I know what pineapple is," Ryan said. "It just doesn't make sense. How do all the dread know what's happened to Lyle?"

She leaned in close and whispered in his ear. "Maybe someone told them."

Ryan rolled his eyes and shook his head. "Never mind." He stared into the sky, watching the battling ships. "If only the coppers and the irons knew the dread were in the middle of a civil war, maybe they could cooperate long enough to launch an offensive all the way out here."

Shay gave Ryan a sly smile. "You're a sneaky mouse. You'd make a devious little mouse king, wouldn't you?"

"Or maybe the dread will kill one another on their own," Ryan mused. "That could work too."

Shay inhaled a deep breath through her nose and then shook her head. "Nope. Smells like a new mouse king to me."

"You seem awfully sure of that."

Shay gave him a confident shrug. "Before scritches ever knew how to make new scritchlings, I made lots and lots and lots of them with my very own two paws. And a mama mouse knows her mouselings."

Jed

The vision faded, and Jed was back, the empty can of green beans still in his hands.

What just happened? It was like he had become that girl . . . *Shay*.

"I escaped from them," he said aloud. "And now they're looking for me."

The first whisperer in his head had said that they were dangerous. But the man didn't seem dangerous at all. The girl, maybe. But neither was angry that he'd left. Only worried.

More sealed memories jiggled in Jed's head, itching to open. There was something about the face of that man and the voice of the girl that had sparked recognition. He focused on the man's face, straining his memory. It felt so close.

The whisperer said they'd stolen him, but Jed didn't know who to trust. The voices in his mind and the visions in his eyes made him wonder if he could even trust himself. Clutching his head in both hands, Jed's thoughts jumped from Ryan to Shay to the mouse king. What did that last one mean? He pictured a giant furry mouse scurrying over the junk, eating passersby.

Nothing made sense. If he could just remember *something. Anything.*

Unsure of what else to do, he stood and kept walking. Another flare lit up in the distance—the lights were getting closer. The longer he walked, though, the more tired he became. *Sleep* . . . he thought. He shook his head to wake himself up. It was too dangerous to sleep here.

Moving onward, he found a dull-red backpack and stuffed it with the few cans of food he found along the way. Even though the backpack was oily, sooty, and worn, the smudge of red made him feel a bit warmer in the gloomy expanse.

Jed's journey forward ended abruptly as he stepped into a puddle of muck that sloshed over his shoe. He pulled his foot back and looked up to see the edge of a river of thick oil. The river cut across his path, bubbling and oozing past in slow motion. It was too wide for Jed to jump across. A bridge of tangled barbed wire, rebar, and chain-link fencing spanned the small gulch to his left. Jed walked to the bridge and tested its sturdiness, putting one foot down and slowly adding more weight before fully committing to a step. The rebar groaned, and the chain link rattled. He wanted to steady himself with the handrails, but barbed wire spiraled around them.

Why would a bridge have handrails covered in barbs?

Jed watched the oil course beneath him. *Can people float in oil?* He thought of the golden gears spinning inside his chest. He'd probably sink.

A nip of pain stung his palm. He jerked his hand away from the barbed railing. The sensation brought back a memory of sitting at the doctor's office while a nurse sewed his skin back together. *Stitches*, he thought. They were called stitches. But he couldn't remember how his skin had gotten cut in the first place. It was so aggravating—fractions of time surrounded in nothingness.

Bits of junk jutted up from the barren fields on the other side of the bridge. The junk sprouted from the ground like . . . *trees*. Trees made of metal. The closer he got, the more the sprouts of junk looked like a forest, tangled and ragged. He neared the forest's edge, where the metal trees cast wicked shadows below.

Jed turned around. He could either stay out in the open field under the dreadnoughts or enter *this*.

An explosion cracked behind him, and orange dots peppered the skyline.

"I'll take my chances." He stepped over the forest line and entered the maze of shadows. Loose junk crunched under his feet. This wasn't the compact floor of junk of the open plains, and it wasn't a friendly place either. Every few steps, his gaze would snap to a shadow that looked more like a claw than the bent coatrack or crooked shower-curtain rod that it really was.

Forests were supposed to be bright, happy places with

greens, and yellows, and browns. *Weren't they?* This one was the color of menace and the shape of razors. Yet it beckoned him farther away from the plains and deeper inside its quiet obscurity. The forest felt like a wolf pretending to sleep, waiting for someone to step into its jaws.

Even so, Jed moved deeper into the belly of the beast.

After an hour, he came to a bookshelf wedged against a wooden cart. He crawled between them and reached in his backpack for a can of cherry pie filling. He pried the top open and scooped out a blob of red goop.

The first taste held memories of cinnamon and nutmeg, toasted butter and rolled oats. The second bite tasted cheap and sticky. Scoop by scoop, he finished the pie filling. He turned the empty can over in his hands, examining it. There were two rust spots on the bottom. Jed used the screwdriver to scratch a curved line under them. A smiley face.

"It's just you and me," he said to the can. "Against the world. Or whatever this place is." The rusty eyes looked back at him.

"You need a name," he said. "What about . . ." He thought for a moment, and then a girl's name popped into his head. "What about: Sprocket?"

Jed nodded. It fit.

"I don't know what I'm doing, Sprocket," he said to her with a sigh. "I don't even know who I am." An uncomfortable wet fog settled over him. Jed shivered and curled into a ball in the small wedge of space under the bookshelf. His eyes were too heavy to keep open anymore.

"Keep watch while I nap," he said, setting Sprocket beside him, eyes facing out into the iron forest. Sleep trickled into Jed's head. The dark fog melted into crisp green leaves and blue skies stuffed with fluffy clouds. He sat cross-legged under a bright lemon tree. A warm breeze blew over his arms and through his hair. Sunlight baked the soft grass under his feet.

"Warrrm . . ." a voice said beside him.

Jed looked down.

Sprocket was nestled in the plush grass, staring up at him. "Hi, Sprocket," Jed said.

"Warrrm sunnn," Sprocket said. The voice was shaky and metallic. It warbled as it spoke, as if it were new to the idea of speaking.

"It's quite warm," Jed agreed. "I like the sun."

"Yesss. Warrrm sunnn. Niiice."

Jed relaxed into the lemon tree.

A whirr sounded from Sprocket. "Somethinnng . . . not right," she said.

Jed sat up straight in his dream. He scanned the horizon, then looked at Sprocket. "What is it? What do you see?"

Sprocket whirred again. Her metal body rattled with the anxious vibration. "Shadowww spyyy."

Jed studied the meadow, and then he glanced up at the sun. A violet eye stared back at him from the center of the golden ball. The eye pulsed slightly as it watched him. Jed scrambled behind the lemon tree. How had he not seen that eye before? He felt ridiculous hiding behind the skinny tree; the violet eye knew exactly where he was.

"Watching you," Sprocket said, a nervous rattle in her tone. "Hunting you."

Jed slunk lower behind the lemon tree's trunk. The slit of violet in the sun narrowed as if to say, *You can't hide from me.*

The puffy clouds darkened, and the blue sky bled with gray.

"What's happening?"

"Storm coming," Sprocket said. "Darkness."

Jed's eyes snapped open, and the dream vanished. He was still underneath the bookshelf. He shivered in the cold fog, rubbed his eyes, and laughed to himself. "Well, Sprocket," he said, turning to the can, "thanks for keeping watch while I—"

His voice cut out.

The can wasn't facing the way he'd placed her before falling asleep. She was turned around, facing *toward* him, her end tilted upward, and her rust-spot eyes locked on his.

"That's . . ." Jed hesitated. "Umm . . ."

He looked up as if the violet eye from his dream were still in the sky. He turned back to Sprocket. The can stared at him, rust-spot eyes and crooked smile unchanged.

He was *sure* he hadn't faced the can that way before he fell asleep. And now, here she was . . . looking at him.

"Sprocket . . . ?" he said, half wondering if the tin can would speak back. Jed sighed. This was ridiculous. She was just an empty can. *Of course*, she wasn't going to speak back to—

A movement flickered in the corner of his eye—a shadow in the darkness. Jed's heart squeezed and the exposed gears under his shirt purred.

He scanned the black around him.

Get up and keep moving, he told himself.

Jed picked up Sprocket and set her inside his backpack. The gaps in the tall metal pieces around him cast branch-like shadows along the ground as he began walking again. Behind him, something creaked. He spun around and squinted at the quiet shapes.

Nothing.

He held perfectly still.

Something was watching him. He could *feel* it. And the longer he stood there, the more eyes he felt. A blistering heat scorched inside him as unseen eyes opened, one by one, until a hundred of them were staring at him. The heat in his chest sweltered, fueling an overwhelming rush of vulnerability. His head whipped back and forth, staring at the quiet, unmoving ground.

Something is here.

It was as if he could smell the being as plainly as he could smell the oil in the air. He tried to swallow. His throat scrunched tight.

"Who—" he whispered, "who are you?"

Silence.

"Answer me!" he yelled.

Heat flared again inside him, burning the edges of his lungs. He hunched over, clutching his chest.

"What's happening to me?" he said, half whisper, half yelp.

A patch of junk shifted a few paces away.

Jed lurched backward, his eyes fixed on the spot.

The junk was still once again.

Jed waited and watched.

Slowly, the junk moved again, as if something were buried underneath. Hiding.

He took another step back. His heel caught on a pipe and he fell. His head struck the ground, and pain crackled through his skull. His vision bounced unsteadily as he scrambled to his feet. Before he could gather his bearings, another patch—this one to his left—began to swell. A third spot wriggled to his right.

Jed ran in the only direction he could—deeper into the forest. He leaped over tangles of pipe and ducked under broken scaffolding. Faster and faster, he moved through the gnarled branches until he reached a clearing walled in by metal foliage and barricades. His breath wheezed and his chest burned with purpose. He collapsed as the fire in him burned hotter still; the eyes found him once again. He squeezed his own eyes shut, but he could still feel them all—the eyes . . . finding him . . . watching him . . . pulling closer.

"Leave me alone!" he yelled.

Jed forced his eyes open and lifted himself up. A flurry of shapes crawled over the ground.

He staggered left, then right.

No matter which direction he went, junk squirmed around him. Again, he tried to run, but something burst free in front of him. A circular saw spun through the junk. Jed shifted direction. The saw flew into the air and soared toward him. Jed fell sideways, and the blade crashed into a filing cabinet.

More junk bubbled up, blocking his path. He jumped over

wires and landed on a stove. Orange light glowed from the burner coils. The heated rings pressed into Jed's arm. He jerked away only to fly into a sewing machine running full throttle.

Everything was *alive*.

A rubber wheel dragged an axle. A washing machine drum crashed against the piles. A blender's blades spun at his feet. Loose bolts shot at him like bullets.

The eyes . . . all of them . . . all around . . . all watching *him*.

"Get away from me!" he yelled. "Stop!"

Immediately, the sewing machine slowed. The stove coils dimmed. The saw blade quieted. The blender's whine died. The rubber wheel stopped turning. The flying hunks of metal fell to the ground.

Jed didn't move. He didn't breathe. The world was silent once again. In the quiet, still, the eyes watched him and waited, expecting him to speak again.

The blender sat motionless at his feet. Jed crouched in front of it—finding the invisible eyes. He reached toward them, and the ember in his chest flared.

The blender's steel blades rotated slowly.

He inched his hand closer.

The blades spun faster.

Another inch.

Faster.

The heat in him burned brighter until the blender was whining once again at full speed.

"Stop," he said, dropping his hand.

The fire in his chest disappeared, and the blender fell silent.

He stared at his hand as if seeing it for the first time. The same question burned inside him: *Who am I?*

This time, something answered: *The key.*

Jed took Sprocket from his backpack, set her on the ground, then picked up the blender. He smashed away the glass until all that was left were blades and motor. He wrenched a spade from the iron forest next and used bootlaces to lash the base of the blender to the shovel's wooden handle.

He assumed a defensive posture and tested the makeshift spear in his grip, spinning it in a circle and jabbing at the empty air.

"How about this?" he asked, glancing down at Sprocket.

Jed imagined the heat in his chest. He concentrated on the blender tip, willing it to spin.

"Go."

Red warmth flared inside of him, but the blender didn't move.

Instead, a tire jerked beneath his feet, sabotaging his battle-stance and pulling his legs out from under him. "Not *you*," he said, kicking the tire. He focused on the blender-spear. "I meant *you*. Now, go." More heat built inside him. This time, the heat felt . . . *blue*.

Again, the blender remained still, but the engine at his feet grumbled to life. It coughed up black puffs of smoke.

"Wow. Useless."

He steadied himself, focusing intensely on the blender.

"Go!"

More blue heat burned within him, but this time, at last, the blades at the end of the spear whirred a few rotations.

"Faster."

He reached for the smoldering fire inside him, trying to spark it into a flame again. But with each attempt, less heat coursed through him and fewer machines responded. He was empty. Depleted. Cold.

Jed studied the weapon in his hands. "At least the blender tip *looks* sort of dangerous, doesn't it?" he asked Sprocket. He slumped down next to the can, considering her. "You're going to need better eyes. Those rust spots aren't going to do."

He pulled a toy Ferris wheel from a heap of junk and unscrewed two bolts. They were different sizes—one dime-size, and the other, nickel-size. "Better than rust spots, I guess." He punched holes through the rust spots and then finagled Sprocket's new bolts into place.

"There," he said with a nod. "Those look much better."

His own eyes flickered again. The iron forest disappeared in a blink.

Shay

Ryan's head wiggled back and forth as he studied the oily, smashed ground.

He looked up at Shay. "Which way now?" he asked.

Shay tapped her chin like a detective. She liked detectives. Lyle once gave her a book that was *all* about them. After reading the book, she found a big magnifying glass without even one crack in it. But she still needed a special hat. The kind that looked like two hats—one pointing front, and one pointing back. And she needed a scoopy, curly pipe to hang in the corner of her mouth. An *extra*-big pipe.

Ryan's face grew more wrinkles the longer he stared at Shay. She didn't like these wrinkles. They weren't the happy kind that peeked out from his cheeks when he smiled. They were ugly, squiggly ones that made his forehead look like a crumpled-up sock.

Shay didn't know where Jed was. Not at all. But she didn't like the wrinkles, so she decided to say something to make them go away.

"Hmm . . ." she said, tapping her chin extra confidently. "Looks like we're getting closer."

"Really?" His ugly wrinkles disappeared, and a couple not-ugly wrinkles smiled from his mouth. "How can you tell?" His head bobbled again as he stared at the ground.

"Well . . . Broken Mouse's scamperings scampered *all about* the Scritcherdom City. Like 'fraidy pitter-pats. Some close—like the shuffles of a sneaky mouse. Some not very close at all—like the scurryings of a lost mouse. Some far, far apart—like the runnings-away of a too-scared mouse. See?"

New wrinkles appeared. Study wrinkles. Not so ugly . . . but not very pretty either.

That's fine. Study wrinkles are okay.

"Oh . . ." Ryan studied the ground more, looking for scamperings. "You think he's scared?"

"Maybe. Maybe not. But he knows Scritcherdom City better than all the other mice. It was his home once. Home sweet home."

Ryan made a wincey look with ugly wrinkles that Shay hadn't ever seen before.

Then his face hardened into determination. "Which direction should we head?" he asked.

Shay felt torn. On the one paw, she didn't like scowly,

worried, 'fraidy wrinkles. Determined Mouse seemed like better company than 'Fraidy Mouse. But, on the other paw . . . she didn't like wasting time scampering about senselessly. She had no idea where Jed was, and if she kept pretending she did, Ryan would turn back into 'Fraidy Mouse and eventually become Frustrated Mouse. Shay had never met a frustrated mouse she'd liked—especially ones frustrated with *her*.

"The trail's gone cold," she said in her best detective squeak.

"Huh? But you just said—"

"But I have an idea. We need to go back to the boat."

"Why?"

"Because boats are faster than Broken Mice, aren't they? We can find him from the sky!"

Ryan nodded. "That sounds like a good plan. We won't be spotted since it's already a dreadnought raft, but those skies"—he gazed nervously at the warring ships in the distance—"they're not safe at all."

"Okay, then, shipmate," she said with a nod. She tried to remember some other boat words, and—with hands on her hips—said to Ryan in her most confident squeak, "Swab the starboard and weigh anchor to the helm sails. We hornswaggling junk-lubbers have got a Broken Mouse to ahoy!"

Jed

Why are they looking for me? Jed wondered, snapping back to himself. They didn't seem like thieves, but then again, Jed didn't know anything about anyone. Shay and Ryan could be thieves, or the whispering voice could be a liar.

"I guess you're the only one I can trust," he said to Sprocket.

Unsatisfied with his companion's half-finished look, Jed pulled two metal hoses from a toppled-over washing machine. He punched four holes in Sprocket's midsection—two on either side of the bottom half, and two on either side of the top half. Then he pushed one of the metal hoses clear through the top set of holes and the second hose through the bottom set. When he was done, Sprocket looked a bit like a four-legged spider.

"There. In case you want to crawl around a bit," Jed said with a smirk.

He placed the tin can on a fallen telephone booth and then surveyed the junk. "What are we doing out here?" he sighed.

Knowing he had no choice, Jed fastened Sprocket to his backpack and then stepped deeper into the iron forest. The farther he walked, the colder he felt. The dark dome of fog overhead made the world forever night. No matter how much time passed, the darkness remained.

"I can't tell if it's actually cold here, or if it's just me," he said to Sprocket. "It's like the cold is coming straight from my bones." He touched his arm and his skin felt chilled. "What's wrong with me, Sprocket?" He glanced back at her, tied atop his backpack, her bolt eyes staring back at him, and he wavered. "I think I need to lie down."

Jed found the guts of a box spring leaning against a tractor. Half of the springs were missing from the skeleton of the bed. He set down his backpack and tried propping the box spring up like a hammock between the tractor and a dresser, but the moment he lay down, the old springs squeaked and snapped. Jed fell through the middle of the frame and landed hard on his back. Again.

He groaned. "You didn't see that, did you?" He glanced at his backpack, and Sprocket's bolt eyes were aimed right at him.

Jed was embarrassed, as if the tin can *had* seen him fall.

He lay there in pain, shutting his eyes. In the blackness, he tried pulling a single, clear face to his mind. Each time a face began to appear, though, a waxy smudge swirled over the image, erasing it. "I just want to go to sleep," he said, "and wake up to memories and faces. Is that too much to ask?"

Sprocket didn't answer, so Jed clambered to his feet with resignation and began walking once again.

The shovel-blender-spear felt heavier the deeper he went into the forest. He half considered chucking it into a tangle of fencing, but holding the spear made him feel a bit safer. Hesitantly, he tried to reach the heat in his chest again and bring life to the blender, but there was no fire left. There was only emptiness and cold.

So tired.

Steps turned into shuffles, and Jed slowly ground to a stop. *So very tired . . .*

He collapsed into an empty bathtub.

His mind drifted off as the blackness of the forest faded into the color of dreams.

He was still in the bathtub, but the bathtub was the size of a tugboat, and it was filled with batteries and food. Meats, fruits, pastries, and cheeses enveloped him in a sea of nostalgia. Bright lemons in a bowl. Warm bread in a basket. A platter of pork roast. He closed his eyes and inhaled. *Apple juice . . . rosemary . . . nutmeg . . . and black licorice?*

Nubs of black licorice sprouted from the roast. He pinched one and plucked it from the meat. Before he could pop it into his mouth, a lemon turned and looked at him. It had a single, violet, glowing eye, pulsing slowly.

"Who are you?" he asked, dropping the licorice and stepping backward.

"I've found him," the lemon said to no one in particular.

"What?"

The lemon spoke again. "He seems physically intact, though his core appears to have been reset. He likely used the Awakening Key as you suspected. His mainframe has been rebooted."

"What's going on?" Jed asked. "Tell me who you are. Why are you watching me?"

The lemon didn't answer.

Instead, Sprocket's voice spoke beside him. "She's snnneaky."

Jed looked at Sprocket, who was balancing on his shoulder. Her bolt eyes stared at him, head cocked.

"Who's watching me?" Jed asked her. "Whose eye is that?"

"Wake up and seee," Sprocket said.

Jed's eyes opened to find a single violet eye staring at him through the jumble of metal branches. The eye pulsed steadily and then blinked. He scrambled out of the bathtub and backed up a few steps. Dim light trickled into the clearing, and a creature emerged. It was metallic—sleek, elegant, and shiny—with bars of steel, copper, and brass woven together perfectly. A dread. But it wasn't like the other dread he'd seen. It was cleaner, crisper, and brighter. It hovered in the air, just inches above the junk floor. Thin wings hummed on its back.

"Who are you?" Jed asked, his voice shaking.

"It appears you were right," the creature said. It had a soft, female voice. "He hasn't recovered his memories yet. The Awakening process is still under way." She waited, as though listening to a response only *she* could hear. "Very well," she said with a nod. "I'll collect him."

She floated forward, her violet eye still watching him.

"Get back," Jed said, raising his arm.

Red heat flared in his chest. Hundreds of pieces of junk in front of him shot at the dread, zapping his energy. The dread sucked in a startled breath and rolled out of the way. Cold replaced the heat inside of Jed instantly.

"Sir," the dread said, fear in her tone. "He's activated the spark. Orders?" She paused. "Aye, sir. I'll bring him."

The dread faced him. Jed stood his ground. He was done running from this thing. "I said, get back."

He drew on the last remnants of power inside his chest. A flurry of junk bombarded the hovering creatures.

She cursed and tried to dodge the whirlwind of metal scraps.

Jed emptied the last of his energy until the woman flew away in retreat. A deep chill overtook him. His vision wobbled and darkened. Voices overlaid the sounds of crashing metal, and he slipped completely into Shay's eyes.

Shay

Shay spotted the yellow lemon tree sprouting from the center of their raft, and she marched toward it confidently, Ryan on her heels.

"Almost there," she said.

"How far do you think we'll get before we're shot out of the sky?" Ryan asked.

Shay shrugged nonchalantly. "Maybe far. Maybe not."

As they neared the lemon tree, Ryan dropped down onto one knee. "Shay," he whispered. "Stop. Look." He pointed to a squad of scritchlings, who were investigating the tree closely.

"Lyle's gotta be around here somewhere," one of them said gruffly. "This is some of his dirt treasure."

Shay smirked. "You're only seeing them now? You need to open your eyes. I've seen them for a mile."

"Then why are we heading toward them?"

"Don't worry. Scritchlings listen to me. They have to do what I say. Don't you remember? I made them." She considered Ryan. "But *you* should be careful; they won't listen to you. They'll turn *you* into soup."

"Soup?"

"Slurpy soup. With engine oil and paprika."

"Yeaaah," Ryan said, drawing the word out. "I'm pretty sure we're not going to go talk to a pack of stray dread. That's probably the worst idea I think I've heard in—"

"Ohhh, scritchbugs," Shay called in a singsong voice, waving her arms. "Over here!"

"Really?" Ryan whispered. "Are you kidding me?"

She cupped her hands to her mouth. "I have some scritcherly questions for you."

The dread immediately turned their attention from the raft. Half of them cocked their heads in confusion as Shay skipped forward.

"You," one of the scritches said, recognizing her face. "The admiral's pet."

"*Former* admiral," another scritch corrected.

"More like *traitor* admiral," a third mumbled.

"Guess he could be both," a fourth said.

"Quiet," the first snapped. "You," he said again to Shay.

Shay nodded once. "Yes. Me. I'm here. And I have four,

maybe five questions." She paused and thought for a moment. "No, maybe six or seven questions to ask you scritchbugs. Or maybe eight. Six if we're lucky. Or seven."

"You're as annoying as these three," the first scritch said. "We don't take orders from little *princesses* any more, girly. Not since the new cap'n took control."

Shay's eyes lit up and she turned to Ryan. "See! See! I told you I could smell it. There's a new mouse king." She sighed in satisfaction before turning back to the scritchling. "Here are my questions: First, do you have any crackers? I'm nibbley."

The scritchling gave her a wicked smile. "We told you. We don't listen to you no more."

"Since when?"

"Since your daddy shot one of our dreadnoughts right out of the sky. We don't follow murderous captains unless they're murdering *not* dreads."

Shay folded her arms. "I don't like him any more than you, but that's definitely not what happened."

The dread shrugged. "Sure looked like that's what happened. And I ain't gonna take the word of some broken *toy* like you."

Heat rushed into Shay's cheeks. *Broken toy? Who does this little scritchwhelp think he's talking to?*

But Lyle had taught her not to lose her temper with peasant mice, so Shay took a deep breath and spoke again. "Then who do you take orders from? Who's the new mouse king?"

The dread puffed out his chest proudly. "Name's Captain Swillface Clunkrucket."

"That's ridiculous," Shay scoffed. "I'd never follow a scritchmouse with a name like that."

"No one never asked a broken toy like you to follow him. Cap'n Clunkrucket's gonna clean things up. Gonna scrape the yard spic and span. Get rid of little whiners and flesh bags. But first, he's gonna find your slippery little daddy. Clunkrucket's gonna take that coward dread king and boil him in oil."

"Listen," Shay said matter-of-factly. "Boiling him in oil simply won't work. His mouse bones are much too goldeny. You'll need something *much* hotter. Much, much hotter. Maybe . . ." She tapped her chin and stared off into the sky. "Maybe engines! Engines are much hotter than boiling oil. Yes, engines. Hot engines. The fiery kinds that go *whooosh!*" She nodded to herself. "Definitely those kinds."

The dread gave Shay a twisty-faced look, unsure of whether she was serious or not. "Well, Clunkrucket's gonna boil you, too, so . . ." He seemed as if he wanted to sound threatening, but all of the confidence was gone from his squeak.

"Deal," Shay said. "I agree to be boiled."

The dread's twisty look got twistier. "Huh?"

"But first"—she held up a finger—"I need your help. We must find a mouse named Jed. Let's talk to Mr. Swillface and see if he has any ideas."

Ryan chittered nervously. "Shay," he squeaked. "Mind if I speak to you . . . *alone?*" Shay turned around. 'Fraidy Mouse continued in a low whisper. "What are you doing?" he asked.

Shay folded her arms. "If you're going to find Broken

Mouse, then you need to learn to be brave, or we're not going to find him at all."

"There's a difference between bravery and *insanity*," 'Fraidy Mouse said.

Shay lifted an eyebrow. "Broken Mouse told me about SPLAGHETTI." Ryan opened his mouth wide enough to fit a whole block of cheese in it. "What does the *I* stand for again?" she asked with an *I know exactly what it stands for, and so do you* tone to her voice.

"Insanity," he mumbled. "But that's not what I—"

Before he could finish, Shay faced the dread and put her hands on her hips. "Where were we?" she asked.

"What did that fleshy bag say?" the dread asked, glaring at Ryan.

"He said he'd like to be boiled in oil as well. Now take us to Mr. Swillface Clunkrucket so we can get on with it."

The first scritch nodded to one of the others, who grabbed a bundle of ropes and began looping them around Shay's wrists.

Shay sighed as she watched the process and then shook her head. "No, silly scritch." She held up her bound wrists. "You're doing it wrong."

"Huh?" The scritch stopped mid-loop.

"You can't just go around and around. Bendy mice can wriggle free." She twisted her hands back and forth and side to side until her hands slipped free. "See?"

The fumbly scritch looked from her hands to the tangle of rope on the ground. "Um . . ."

"Try again," she said, "but this time, go around and around, crisscross, crisscross. Then around and around, crisscross, crisscross again. Okay?"

Shay scooped up the rope, untangled it, and handed it back to Fumbly Scritch. His face squinched awkwardly, as if he weren't sure whether to be angry, embarrassed, or maybe even a little appreciative. He assessed the rope and then assessed her wrists.

"Around and around, crisscross, crisscross," Shay prompted helpfully.

Fumbly Scritch nodded to himself as he looped the rope around and around, then crisscrossed twice.

"Perfect," Shay said, giving Fumbly Scritch an encouraging smile. "See?" She held up her wrists, twisting them back and forth. "Nice and tight. And you got it on your first try. I think you might just have a talent for tying up prisoners. That's a useful skill. And useful skills are good—especially for scritchmice."

Fumbly Scritch's back straightened a few inches in pride as he admired the ropes around Shay's wrist. "You think so?"

"Absolutely. Now give it another try on this mouse." She motioned to Ryan.

"Around and around, crisscross, crisscross," Fumbly Scritch whispered to himself.

Jed

Jed's own vision swirled back into focus. He was lying on his back in the iron forest. Scraps of metal covered him in a messy pile.

He pushed the loose junk away and sat up. He looked around, but the violet-eyed woman was gone.

"SPLAGHETTI," he whispered to himself, the vision still fresh in his mind. The word conjured up more memories of a home he once lived in. It had meant something important . . . something he needed to survive. He tried focusing on the other things he'd seen in his vision. The dread had mentioned that there was a new dread king. Swillface Clunkrucket. Jed pictured a gnarled face atop a monstrous body with four arms and twenty feet tall.

Unsettled, Jed climbed back to his feet, retrieved his blender-spear, and continued walking. The forest was a wash of black and gray. He scanned the metal for the glowing dot of violet light.

The tightly packed junk made a slight crinkly sound as his shoes pressed against it. It was a steady, predictable sound that only made him more tired the longer he walked.

Step, crunch.

Step, crunch.

Step, crunch . . . crunch.

Jed froze. He pointed the blender-spear in the direction of the extra crunch. "Who's there?"

Another crunch sounded to his right, and a third behind him. Finally, he saw pinpricks of light.

Eyes.

Watching him.

But these eyes were different. They were red, not violet.

Creatures shifted in the shadows. A face of wires and gears peeked through a gap in the forest. Brackets and bolts bound old skin to metal plates. Its left eye socket was filled with nails. Its right socket held a red eye a few sizes too big for its face.

"Well, hello, secret boy," it said, licking its bottom lip quickly as if it had a tongue like a lizard. "All alone, are we? No dread king anymore. No orders to not slurp up secret boys. Secret boys smell so good. So tasty."

Jed aimed the blender-spear at the creature. "Back away," he said as confidently as he could manage.

The creature looked at the spear and assessed the blender

at its tip. "Is secret boy a trickster boy?" It took a wary step back, as if recognizing something for the first time. But then it waited, as if expecting an answer. "Well? Is secret boy a trickster boy, too?"

"What are you talking about?" Jed asked.

It pointed at the blender. "That. You make it go? Buzz, spin, crunch, shrieking dread. Can you make dread be shrieking dread?" The dread's expression changed from fearful to eager.

"Yes." Jed nodded slowly. The creature's eye widened. "I can make it go."

"Do it," the creature said, his whole body shaking with excitement. "Do it, do it, *do it*!" His tongue tapped his top lip rapidly, and he squirmed with anticipation.

Jed reached for any warmth still left in his body. "Go," he whispered to the blender. It didn't move. "Go," he said louder. But the fire inside him was gone. He had nothing left. "Go," he shouted at the blades. Nothing.

The creature writhed with frustration and expectation. The longer Jed failed to bring life to the blender, the more frustrated the creature became. "Liar! Liar, liar, *liar*! Wicked little cheat!"

"No," Jed said, insistent. "I can. I can make it go."

"Secret boys are cheaty little liars that can't make any things go!" It cocked its head and looked at Jed hungrily. "I heard," it said, glancing at other dark shapes around them, "that secret boys are filled with sparkly treasure."

"*Lots* of sparkly treasure," another creature said to Jed's left.

"I want sparkly treasure," a third said excitedly. "I want to pull it all out of him."

All of the dread began to nod. Some licked their lips. Others began to tremble with excitement.

Jed could see the attack in the creature's hunched posture—its shoulders high and face forward, a skulking wolf ready to kill.

Metal clanked all around him.

At first, it was just one set of footsteps, and then it was two . . . then three. Soon, all around him, footsteps crunched against loose junk.

He was surrounded. The circle of dread began to close in on him, constricting on all sides until they were only a few leaps away.

"Get away from me!" Jed yelled, swinging the blender-spear.

"Slurp him to bits!" The creatures dove for Jed, arms outstretched, mouths gaping open.

Jed

Jed lifted his blender-spear and gritted his teeth. A hand gripped the back of his shirt. He swung his spear, though he knew it was pointless to resist. There were too many of them. The grip on his shirt tightened and pulled. Jed braced himself to be yanked into the mob. But the hand didn't pull him backward. It pulled him *up*.

His feet left the ground, and he rose into the sky.

Iridescent wings fluttered above him. They were long and thin and beat quickly. The wings were attached to an elegant, mechanical flyer with the single violet eye. Now that Jed could see, he could tell it had the shape of a woman, though most of her face had been replaced by gears. She gripped him tightly, hovering just out of reach from the dread below.

The woman flew higher, struggling to lift them both. Her iridescent wings beat faster, forming a ghostly blue-green-purple-gold blur.

"Who are you?" Jed called up to her.

"That's classified," she said.

"Huh?"

The dread swarmed under them in a horde. The woman strained to gain height. "Are you okay?" Jed asked.

She held out a chain with her free hand. "Wrap this around your waist," she said.

He did so, and she used a carabiner to clip the chain links securely. She let go of Jed's shirt. He fell a few inches, but the chain snapped taut and held the two together in the air.

One of the dread swung a pipe at his ankle. Jed yelped and the woman lifted them higher. Shadows of dread flickered through the metal below. "What's going on?" Jed asked. "Why are they trying to kill me?"

"That's classified."

"Fine. Then where are you taking me? And don't tell me that's classified, too."

"That's classified, too."

"I'm not blindfolded. It's not like you're going to be able to hide the answer for long."

She glanced down, assessing him as if wondering whether or not she should put a blindfold on him. "Stop talking already," she said.

The dread below piled on top of one another trying to reach them. "It doesn't look like they're giving up," he said.

"Astounding observation. Apparently, you're just as brilliant as he said you'd be."

"Who?" Jed waited for an answer, but she ignored him. "That *who* said I'd be?" he repeated.

She glanced down and her violet eye glinted in the dim light. "Let's play a little game while we fly for our lives, shall we? Here's how it goes: You ask me a question, and I say 'classified.' Do the rules make sense? Or should I explain them again?" When he didn't respond, she nodded.

Her wings whined under the strain of his weight and fluttered faster to compensate. Jed and the woman flew above the forest away from the horde. At the edge of the forest, the junk dropped off over a sharp edge into nothingness.

"Is that . . . is that a *cliff*?"

There was no response, of course.

They reached the cutoff, and only then could Jed see the other side of the chasm in the distance. As they crossed over the gorge, the wings slowed, and they plunged into the darkness of the ravine.

"Are we supposed to be falling?" Jed asked.

"Maybe you could try not talking until we land," she said through a strained voice.

"By 'land,' you don't by chance happen to mean 'crash at the bottom of this gulch,' do you?"

"Would you just shut up already?" Her voice was as tight as the tension in her face.

Behind them, the dread had piled near the ridge of the cliff. They shouted down at them, hurling pipes and cans in

his direction. Some slipped and fell into the darkness. Bits of metal burst into pieces as dread hit the bottom.

Jed feared the woman's wings would fizzle out completely. As they slowly fell, Jed made out movement below them.

Liquid. Black and shiny.

Oil.

A great river of oil snaked along the canyon walls.

"We're almost there," the woman said. Smoke slithered up behind the gears in her back, leaving a white trail of overheated strain. She pointed to a dry bank of land on the other side of the chasm, untouched by the coursing oil.

A pop sounded from her wings and she winced. "You may want to brace yourself. This won't be comfortable." The gears in her back grinded to a halt, and her wings sputtered to a stop. The two fell from the sky and hit a bank of dry ground.

Jed rolled over and shifted his arms and legs to make sure they weren't broken. He unclipped the carabiner and unwrapped the chain from around his chest, then checked on Sprocket, still tied to his backpack. She was a bit dented but mostly intact.

"Thanks," Jed said at last. "You probably saved my life."

The woman sat up. "No, I *definitely* saved your life. You were one second away from getting slurped by dread."

"*Dread.* What are those things?"

She squinted at him. "You're kidding, right?"

He shifted uncomfortably. "Not exactly."

"You don't know what dread are?" She laughed once and motioned to the world around them. "How can you not know what they are? You're smack in the middle of the fog. Who the clunk lives here and doesn't know what a dread is?"

Jed smiled. "That's classified."

"And thinks he's funny, too, huh? You'd better be worth it. Since, because of you, now every dread on the barge knows where our base is."

Jed looked around. He didn't see a base—just more smashed-up junk. "What base?"

He waited for another snide *That's classified* remark, but instead the woman simply pointed to a series of train cars embedded into the junk a dozen feet above them.

"I'm Alice, by the way," she said, still sitting on the ground.

"Nice to meet you. I'm . . . well, I don't really know who I am."

"Admiral said you might have forgotten a bit. I didn't realize how much."

Jed's heart jittered in his chest. "So you know who I am?" Jed asked.

Alice shrugged. "Maybe."

He waited, but she didn't say anything else. "What . . . what's my name?" he asked.

"That's classified," she said with a wink.

Jed ground his teeth together and glared at her. "Right."

"I'm kidding. But I'm still not going to tell you."

"What? Why? It's *my* name. I'm pretty sure I have a right to know it." Anger leaked into the words as he said them.

"Sorry. Not my place. You'll have to ask the admiral. I'm supposed to find you and bring you here. That's all.

Admiral said very specifically that *he* would answer all of your questions—and no one else."

Jed folded his arms and surveyed the train car above them. "Fine. If you're not going to tell me, then take me to this admiral."

"That's the mission. He's been waiting a long time to see you."

The gears on Alice's back began to turn once again, and her wings briefly fluttered, lifting her upright. Before her feet left the ground, the grinding returned, and smoke coughed from the engines. The wings twitched and stopped, and Alice fell back down. "Hmm . . ." she said. "You go on ahead. I'll be right behind."

"It doesn't look too far up," Jed said. "I'm sure we could just climb instead of fly."

"Just go. I already told you; I'll be right there."

"Why won't you come with me?" Jed realized that Alice hadn't stood since the crash. "Are you okay? Did you get hurt when we landed?"

"That landing felt like I was a slug getting kicked by a wrench. Of course I got hurt. But I'm fine. Now get going."

Jed walked over and held out his hand. "Here, let me help you up."

She clamped her teeth together, and her violet eye looked away. "Look. My legs don't exactly work like other legs. And by that, I mean they don't. *Work*, that is. Got it? I can't walk, okay?"

"Oh. Sorry. I didn't mean to . . ."

Alice rolled her eyes. "Stop looking at me like that."

"Like what?"

"All droopy-faced. Your eyes look like melting butter. In case you don't remember, I can fly. And you can't. What do I need legs for when I can fly?" She reached both arms in front of her and dragged herself forward a few feet. "Go," she said motioning to the train car. "Have Zix give you the tour. I'll catch up."

Jed searched for an entrance. "Where do I—"

"Third window from the left. Knock twice. Pause. Then twice again." He waited for her to catch up, but she waved him forward. "Didn't I just tell you to stop it with the pity treatment? I'll be fine. Now get going. They're all waiting for you."

He wanted to ask *who* was waiting for him, but instead he walked the few steps to the steep canyon wall of junk. He wedged his foot on the edge of a mixing bowl and lifted himself up to a cuckoo clock. From there, he climbed to the train car jutting out from the junk. He scooted to the third window. The glass was scratched and blurry.

He knocked on the window twice, then twice again.

"Who is it?" a muffled voice called from inside.

Jed wasn't sure how to answer. "I don't know exactly."

"Huh? You don't know who you are?"

"Yeah. I guess."

"What kind of clunk head doesn't know who they—"

"Zix," Alice called from below. "Open up. It's the boy. I got him. And hurry. He brought dread with him."

A pair of latches clicked loose from inside, and the window slid open. There was Zix. Another winged machine. Dull metal weaved cleanly through his face, held together with small bolts and oiled hinges. Instead of eyes, Zix had two metal hoses extending from his eye sockets. At the end of each hose were solid green lights. Small shutters blinked open and shut over the lights.

"Hmm," he said. "So, you're the one?"

"The one *what*?" Jed asked.

"That's him," Alice called.

"Well get in here already," Zix said. "Admiral wants to have a look at you."

The window slid shut, and a door Jed hadn't noticed yet opened in front of him. Jed stepped into what appeared to be a passenger cabin. A pair of bunk beds ran along each side wall, and there was a small table in between them with playing cards left facedown. Two other winged figures sat across from one another, fanned-out cards in their hands.

"Welcome on board the *Endeavor*. Finest crew of dragonflies you'll find in the whole yard," Zix said. His wings twitched as he considered what he'd just said. "Well . . . I suppose we're the *only* dragonflies you'll find in the yard. We're a specialty squad of sorts, but this rig hasn't been operational for years, so we're scrambling to get it running as fast as possible. Some dragonflies were even still in hibernation."

"Hibernation?"

"Sure. Just like you. The admiral told us you've been powered down for the last three weeks. Didn't know if he'd ever find you again, but then your signal popped up a few days ago and Alice has been looking for you ever since."

Three weeks . . . Jed thought to himself. *I've been asleep for three weeks?* The fuzzy memories made it feel like three *years* instead of three weeks.

"Alice is the newest member of the crew," Zix continued. "She joined about a month ago."

"Hey," the dragonfly closest to Jed said. "Does Brindle got that jack of hearts in his hand? Take a peeksies for me, will you?"

The dragonfly across from him scowled and hunched over his cards.

"This here's Dak, and that there's Brindle," Zix said.

Dak was a tank with wings. His thick metal body was plated in shiny strips of steel held together with meaty bolts. Brindle, on the other hand, was a flimsy, jointless bundle of copper wire.

Brindle noticed Jed's stare. "It's so I can move better." He set his cards on the table and flung his arms back and forth. The bundled wires had impressive flexibility, rotating in a full circle at the elbows. *They look like spaghetti,* Jed thought.

No . . . not spaghetti . . . SPLAGHETTI. It was that word again, the one from the vision. It hovered in his mind. SPLAGHETTI . . . What was SPLAGHETTI? It was something important—something that he was supposed to have with him. Something that would save his life. But his pockets were empty. His backpack only had a few cans of food and Sprocket. He didn't have SPLAGHETTI—whatever it was.

Brindle had nearly turned his head all the way around. "Pretty neat, huh?" he said.

Jed nodded, still not able to shake the word SPLA-GHETTI from his mind.

"Stop showing off," Dak said. "You look like a stretched-out slug. And it's your turn to play."

Brindle flushed, and his head swiveled back in place. "You're just jealous," he said, "because your lumbering scrapheap of a body can barely fit through a doorway."

Dak's jaw tightened. He slapped his cards on the table and stood. "How's about I take that rubber-band body of yours and tie it into a little knot? Betcha won't be so smug then, eh?"

Brindle smirked. "You'd have to catch me first. And those wagons you call hands aren't exactly nimble."

"It's a small room," Dak said. "My wagon hands will catch you eventually, and when they do, I'll squish you up so small, you'll fit in my pocket."

Zix sighed. "Just don't break anything, you two. Got it?" He motioned for Jed to follow. "Come on. Let's get you to the admiral."

They stepped into a corridor. "This is the *Endeavor*," Zix said. "Dragonfly headquarters. The admiral is near the back, so you're going to get the short tour. You came by the front of the train toward the helm. To make it easier, we call anything *toward* the helm 'north,' and anything toward the back of the train 'south.' Got it?"

"Got it," Jed said.

Zix nodded. "Good. Follow me. First is the engine room." They entered a humming room filled with gauges, pipes, and pistons. In the center stood a bright orange cylinder taller than Jed, and as wide as a barrel. "This here's the Ion Battery," Zix said. "Admiral's own invention. Fully charged, this beauty will power a whole city. It's a piece of art." He paused for a moment, admiring the battery.

He led them into the next train car. When he opened the door, intense color shone back at Jed in brilliant, rich life. "This is the garden." There were trees with peaches, plums, apples, and lemons. There were strawberry bushes, green bean strands, spearmint bushes, tomato plants, grape vines, and more. The top of the car was a solid sheet of glass. Jed desperately wanted to linger, but Zix dragged him forward.

"Next to the garden, we have the mess hall, naturally." They entered a crew-kitchen and dining area where two winged dragonflies sat, one eating a bowl of tomato soup, and the other biting into an apple. They gave Zix a nod as he passed.

"Then we've got crew cabins for the next four cars. Ten rooms in each car."

On either side of the next corridor were five doors leading into the crew cabins.

After the crew cabins was the medical station they called the med box.

As they passed through the med box, other winged workers toiled busily preparing panels, welding pipes into place, and soldering bits of wire together. Some knelt by panels on the floor, while others hovered near the ceiling, their wings keeping them steady in the air. The gentle hum from the wings was very different than the sandy, grinding sound that Alice's made, as if hers were perpetually just a little bit broken.

"What are they doing?" Jed asked.

"What does it look like they're doing?" Zix said.

"I don't know," Jed said. "Fixing something." But the image seemed off to Jed. He knew that his memory was a pile of scrap, but as far as he could remember, trains didn't have gears and machinery wired so abundantly throughout their frames. "I just didn't know train cars had so many machines inside their walls."

Zix gave him a raised eyebrow. "You don't even know who you are, and suddenly you're an expert on trains?"

Jed shook his head. "That's not what I meant. Sorry."

Zix shrugged. "Next is the ship's workshop."

After the workshop, they passed through a storage locker, and then a fully stocked library. All four walls were floor-to-ceiling bookcases stocked full of leather-bound books. The bookcases were made from rich cherry wood that felt warm and inviting. Yellow light from a single chandelier bathed the wood in a gentle glow. In the middle of one of the side walls, a fireplace burned with a soothing flicker. Two plush, leather chairs sat on either side of a small, round table.

"Finally, we have the admiral's quarters."

Zix opened the next door, which led into a finely decorated cabin. In the corner was a desk made from dark polished wood. Paintings of landscapes hung along the walls. Soft violin music played from an old phonograph.

A man sat in a chair behind the desk sketching something on a blank sheet of paper. He looked up as Jed entered. Black bandages wrapped around his face, covering his features. He wore a formal button-up shirt with a black coat.

Jed couldn't see the man's eyes, but he could feel them locked onto his own. The admiral set down his pen and leaned back in his chair. "You found him. Well done, Alice. Well done, indeed."

"Oh," Jed said. "Alice is actually still outsi—"

But before he could continue, he felt a tap on his shoulder. He turned around. Behind him was Alice—holding herself upright with a handrail on the ceiling—giving him a little wave.

"I told you," she said. "I'm not a toddler. I can get around just fine."

"I'm sure our guest wasn't trying to hurt your feelings when he called you a toddler," the man behind the desk said.

Jed held up his hands and shook his head. "Oh—no, I didn't actually call her a toddler. I was just—"

"I'm kidding," the man said. "I know you didn't. Alice tends to exaggerate."

Alice shrugged. "It's been known to happen."

"Anything interesting to report, Alice?"

"He's heavier than I thought he'd be," she said, massaging her shoulder.

"It's all that gold in him," the man said. The bandages around his mouth dimpled with what looked like a smile. "It's heavier than it looks. Anything else?"

"Just that we're lucky I got to him when I did. A horde was about to slurp him up when I yanked his clunk neck to safety."

"Did they follow you?"

"Yes."

The man nodded. "Tell Zix that we're going to need to move up our time line. Let's get everything finished here within the hour."

"Within the *hour*?" Alice asked. "That's pushing it."

"Well," the man said, "we can either finish within the hour, or all get slurped up together. I'd prefer to stay in one piece, wouldn't you? So, see if you can *encourage* Zix to get it done. Yes?"

Alice nodded and left the room.

The man shifted in his chair. Jed felt him staring through the black bandages. "I see you got my signal."

"You were the one sending the flares," Jed said, realizing that he should have made the connection earlier.

"Yes. My apologies for being a bit *intrusive*, but it's critical that we begin your training as soon as possible."

"My training? Training for what?"

"To save the world, of course."

"I'm pretty sure you have the wrong kid," Jed said. "I don't even know who I am."

"That's all right," he said, "I know enough about you for the both of us."

Jed's heart fluttered in his chest. "You do? What's going on? I woke up, and I didn't know where I was. I didn't know my own name or who the people lying next to me were. And then I heard your voice inside my head. How did you do that? Where am I? What is this place?"

The man patted the air with both hands. "Slow down,"

he said. "I'll answer all your questions soon. Your name is Jed. And you are my son."

"What? You're my *dad*?"

The man nodded. "I built you. A long time ago. And the people you were with, they took you from me. They're dangerous people. But you're safe here now, with me."

"Why can't I remember you? Why can't I remember anything?"

"You must have used the Guardian Key."

"I don't remember," Jed said. "What does it do?"

"You were built to save this world—to act as a guardian for your people. You have special abilities and power locked inside you. The Guardian Key shuts you down to start your powers. Once activated, your body reawakens. All of the gears inside you begin to turn again. The gears in your mind, however, take longer. You will regain your memory. Give it time. But I must emphasize: It is critical that we begin your training immediately."

Jed studied the man. He tried to remember him as his father, but nothing came. "How do I know you're telling me the truth?"

"That's a good question," the man said. "I suppose I don't have a good answer for you, but I've already saved your life twice. That's got to count for something."

"Twice?"

"Once from the kidnappers, once from the dread."

Jed wanted to say Alice actually saved him from the dread, and he wasn't so sure about the kidnappers.

"Why is your face covered?" Jed asked.

"Apologies for this," the man said, touching his cheek. "I was recently injured. I need time to heal." He reached to the back of his head and began unwrapping the bandages. Black gauze fell away until slivers of gold shined through the gaps. He removed the rest of the bandages and smiled at Jed.

Skin covered most of his face, but patches of golden gears spun in his left cheek, jaw, and forehead.

Familiarity churned in Jed. He knew this face.

"I . . . I know you from somewhere," Jed said. He was certain that buried in his memory he'd seen the man. He could almost see his face in . . . in a photograph.

The man nodded. "Of course you do. You're my son."

But the word *son* felt wrong to Jed.

"Let me formally welcome you aboard the *Endeavor*," the man continued. "I am the captain of this rig. The crew calls me Admiral, but you can call me Lyle."

Jed

Jed touched the center of his chest where his skin was still healing over the golden gears. Lyle's face—it *was* made of the same metal as the gold in his chest. Maybe the man was his father, like he said. Jed was convinced that he had a father—something inside him was sure of it—but if it was Lyle, why couldn't Jed remember him?

He walked to the window in Lyle's cabin and stared at the cliffs opposite the *Endeavor*. Ropes dangled like tentacles from the tops of them, descending to a dry bank on the opposite side of the river. Dread slithered down them in swarms, landing on the bank.

Two knocks sounded at the cabin door. Lyle looked up. "Come in," he said.

Zix entered, hands clasped behind his back. One of his green eyes extended and swiveled to look at Jed. The other watched Lyle. "The dread are dropping into the canyon," he said. "They're on their way."

"How many?" Lyle asked.

"I sent Brindle to get a count. He came back reporting a couple thousand—maybe more."

Lyle rubbed his eyes. "Brindle can't count worth scrap," he sighed. "That could mean five hundred or thirty thousand."

Zix nodded. "I know. But you told me that we have one hour. I need my best dragonflies patching the *Endeavor*, not counting dread. And . . . well, Brindle isn't exactly one of my *best*."

"I suppose it doesn't matter anyway," Lyle said. "Five hundred isn't much different than thirty thousand when we're sitting out in the open at the bottom of this gorge."

"What should I tell the crew?" Zix asked.

"Tell them whatever will help get the job done. How many more junk runs do we need to make?"

Zix scrunched his lips to the side and stared up at the ceiling as he ran calculations. "We could use another fifteen runs, to be honest, but I'll bet we could get the bare essentials in four—if we get lucky with the digs. There's a salvage site nearby that might have everything we need. Most of our dragonflies can get there in twenty minutes."

Lyle tapped his chin. "That's forty minutes round trip, which means only fifteen or twenty minutes for installation and wiring."

"I've got a good crew of dragonflies," Zix said. "They'll get it done."

"Make it happen."

Zix nodded once and walked out.

"How are the dread going to get across the river?" Jed asked.

Lyle shook his head. "We'll be fine."

"But if they *do* reach us, what then? A train's boxcar door isn't going to stop them."

"That's true. But, even if it did, I'm guessing a whole fleet of dreadnoughts is on its way—probably from every direction. That horde is the least of our problems."

"Why do all of them want to kill me so badly?" Jed asked.

"It's not you they want," Lyle said. "They are more likely after me."

"Why?"

Lyle sighed. "It's a long story, but the short of it is that I helped create them. I gave them life. They used to think I was their king, but someone's convinced them that I betrayed them and am trying to kill them. Most of them have turned against me and have been hunting me ever since. I created the *Endeavor* in case I ever lost control of them and needed to escape this place . . . which, unfortunately seems to be the case now. . . . I never expected the dread to be able to organize as quickly as they've managed. The *Endeavor* and its crew simply wasn't prepared for this."

"You made those things?" Jed took a step backward, away from Lyle.

"That's an even longer story. But they are wrong; I never

betrayed them. The dread are greedy, and one of them is spreading lies about me to seize control. I've never met the traitor . . . only heard his name."

"Swillface Clunkrucket," Jed said.

Lyle looked up. "How do you know that?"

Jed hadn't meant to speak. The words just fell out of his mouth. "I heard the name, too," he said, his voice more than suspicious.

Lyle squinted, knowing that Jed wasn't telling him everything, but he didn't press the issue. "Yes, Swillface Clunkrucket. He's rallied most of the dread forces."

"How many is that?" Jed asked.

"About thirty battlenoughts, two dozen ghostnoughts, ninety fully armed dreadnoughts, and nearly seventy thousand dread soldiers."

"And none of them follow you anymore?" Jed asked.

"Less than twenty thousand. But nearly all of them are on the front lines trying to hold back Clunkrucket. There's also another ten thousand or so not following anyone and just running around the barge like wild dogs."

"Did you betray them?" Jed asked. "Like Swillface says you did?"

"I didn't shoot down that ship," Lyle said, not really answering the question. "Clunkrucket is a liar."

"And if what you said is true—that he's coming for us—what are we going to do?"

"Let Zix and the dragonflies work on that. You and I have something more important to do."

"What?"

Lyle lightly slapped both of his palms flat on the desk. "Right now, I could really go for some eggs. Are you hungry?"

"Am I *hungry*?"

"I can't imagine you found anything worth eating in a place like this—certainly not eggs. Am I right?"

Jed looked out the window again. "Why does it matter whether I'm hungry or not? You just said a fleet is coming to kill us."

"And there's nothing you or I can do about that. I don't have dragonfly wings to fly for salvage parts, and I'm not a ship's engineer. You and I would just get in the way. So, we can stare out the window at the dread, or we can go make some eggs. Which sounds better?"

Lyle stood and beckoned Jed to follow without waiting for an answer. They entered a new boxcar, accessible through the other end of his cabin.

Once inside, Jed no longer felt like he was in a train. The space had been transformed into a kitchen complete with a double oven, an open range cooktop, warming drawers, pantries, cupboards, and a sink recessed into a small, granite-covered island countertop.

Lyle walked to the stove and turned one of the knobs. It clicked as the igniter sparked. A whoosh of flames danced to life.

"How do you like your eggs?" he asked.

"I don't remember," Jed said.

"Hard-boiled? Soft-boiled? Scrambled?"

Jed shrugged. "I don't know."

"Omelet? Sunny side up? Over easy? Over medium? Over hard? Poached? Baked? Basted? Spanish fried? Coddled? Anything ringing a bell?"

"Sorry."

"Poached it is, then. Grab me a pot, will you?"

Jed lifted a copper pot from the hook hanging above the island and held it out toward Lyle.

"Come on over." Lyle motioned. "I'll show you how to poach an egg. Go ahead and fill the pot half-full of water, add just a splash of vinegar, and set it to a steady simmer." He stepped back and allowed Jed to complete the instructions. "The key," he said as Jed worked, "is fresh eggs. If your egg isn't fresh, it doesn't matter how perfectly you cook it, it won't turn out the way you want."

"Where do you get fresh eggs out here?" Jed asked.

"Not from a can, I'll tell you that much." Lyle's face twisted in disgust. "We don't eat garbage on the *Endeavor*."

He opened a refrigerator door and selected a single egg from a wicker basket. He held the egg in two fingers in front of Jed's face. "The ability to poach an egg says a lot about one's grace. One misstep, and instead of a delicacy, you end up with yolk-flavored water." He tapped the egg once on the granite countertop and a thin line split the shell in two. Then he poured the contents into a small ceramic dish.

Lyle waited for the water to heat up, then he took a metal spoon and swirled the water in a circle until it formed a gentle whirlpool. He carefully poured the egg with its unbroken yolk into the center of the swirling water. The whites of the egg turned with the current and wrapped the yolk in a thin cocoon. After a few minutes, he scooped up the egg with a slotted spoon and waited for the water to drip away before carefully setting it onto a plate.

The egg was beautiful—clean, and white, and a flawless teardrop shape. Lyle grinded two twists of pepper and one twist of salt over the egg, then handed the plate to Jed.

"Tell me what you think," Lyle said.

Jed took a fork and cut into the center. Bright yellow spilled onto the plate. He put the bite on his tongue and an explosion of memory coursed through him. Smoked salmon with cream cheese and lemon, foie gras sorbet, warm lobster benedict, fresh avocados, and tiramisu. A thousand colors and flavors burst through his mouth as if he were tasting them all for the first time—the texture of hazelnut-crusted halibut on his tongue . . . the smell of fresh-baked cinnamon bread in the morning . . . the sizzle of browned butter in a pan.

The sensations were overwhelming. He closed his eyes, drinking in the tastes and smells and memories of a lifetime of food.

"Are you all right?" Lyle asked.

The memories evaporated as Jed was pulled back to the present. He chewed slowly on the poached egg. It wasn't fancy, but it was cooked perfectly, a wonderfully fresh egg, delicately poached and subtly seasoned.

"I remember," Jed said.

A look of hesitation crossed Lyle's face. "Remember what?"

"Food. Every bite I've ever taken."

Lyle smiled. "Now, isn't that much better than watching a horde of ugly monsters gather to try and kill you?"

Jed's stomach tightened at the thought. He nodded uncertainly.

Together, they poached another egg. This time, Lyle letting Jed do most of the work while he made two slices of toast.

Not long after they'd finished eating, a light knock sounded at the door.

"Well," Lyle said, dabbing the corners of his mouth with a napkin, "I suppose it's time to get back to threats of death. Come in," he called.

Zix entered. "We were able to salvage enough from the junk runs to get the ion battery online."

"Power it up. We need to act quickly. If the horde doesn't get to us soon, Clunkrucket's dreadnoughts will."

"Oh," Zix said, his green eyes shrinking back into their sockets, "the horde will get us first."

Jed walked to the window. While he and Lyle had been making eggs, the horde had launched dozens of grappling hooks from their bank into the junk above the *Endeavor*. Hundreds of dread shimmied upside down along the cables toward the train, creeping rapidly along like giant metal spiders.

And the first wave was nearly across the river.

Jed

"They're coming," Jed said. "We have to do something."

Lyle's hand squeezed his shoulder. "You're probably right. I'd say we have about fifteen seconds to figure something out, or we're all dead."

Jed's jaw slackened and his gaze drifted up to meet Lyle's. "Are you—are you serious?"

"Of course I'm not," he said with a half smirk and a wink. "Do you really think I would have spent the last hour in the kitchen if I didn't think we had a plan?"

"Then how are we going to get out of here?" Jed asked, looking for some secret exit.

Lyle gave him a knowing smile. "We're not going anywhere.

The *Endeavor* is." He nodded once to Zix. "Detonate the charges."

Zix nodded and pulled a lever on one of the walls. A series of small popping explosions crackled in the air. Their boxcar teetered slightly and fell a few inches. Dread scrambled aboard, landing on the roof of the train and skittering down the sides toward the entrances. The boxcar's sudden movement shook some off, but others clawed at the metal frame and pounded on the windows. Cracks splintered across the extra-thick glass, angry lines spreading in small clusters.

Lyle lifted his hand. "Full throttle in three . . . two . . . one . . ." He dropped his hand as he spoke the next word. "Now!"

Zix smashed his palm into a large button beside the lever.

The boxcar jolted, and Jed grabbed a handhold to keep from falling.

The *Endeavor* ripped away from the cliff and hovered above the oil river.

Then it began to rise.

Jed scrambled unsteadily to the window and pressed his face against the glass, looking backward and forward. A trail of boxcars hovered in front of him, and just as many hung in the air behind him. The *Endeavor* was a giant stirring snake swaying in place ever so slightly, as if waking from a deep sleep.

Zix cranked more levers, spun dials, flipped switches, and examined meters. "All systems functional. Engines at two percent. Hull holding steady. Ship-wide communication operational."

"*Ship?* This train is a ship?" Jed asked.

Lyle smiled. "Would have been sort of risky hiding out in the bottom of a gorge if she weren't, right?"

"And it can fly?"

"What do you think she's doing right now?"

"I mean, *really* fly."

Lyle motioned to a brass crank and a metal panel filled with holes. "Zix, put me on with the crew."

Zix punched another few buttons, wound the crank, and then nodded. "You're on."

Lyle stepped forward and leaned in next to the metal panel. "Dragonflies of the *Endeavor*, this is your admiral speaking." His voice crackled overhead with a metallic ring. "Let's get off this scrap heap, shall we?" Answering roars echoed from boxcars in front and behind theirs. "Everyone to your stations and stay on high alert until we're clear." He stepped away from the speaker. "Take us out, Zix."

Zix slowly pushed a lever forward. The *Endeavor* inched ahead, drifting over the oil river. "Engines at four percent," he said. "Holding steady. Five percent . . . Six percent . . ."

The ship moved more rapidly the harder Zix pressed the lever. He opened his mouth to continue announcing their progress, but just then, the engines cut out, stopping the ship with a jolt and leaving nothing but silence behind.

Jed's stomach lurched as the *Endeavor* started to drop—slowly at first, and then faster and faster.

"Zix!" Lyle shouted. "What is goin—?"

They hit the oil river with a jarring slap. Zix, Lyle, and Jed crumpled to the ground. The *Endeavor* bobbed in place, floating off-kilter on the thick, oozing surface.

"Main lift thrusters are off-line," Zix said, scrambling to his feet to adjust dials and check meters.

"Reroute engine thrust," Lyle commanded. "Divert power to lift boosters one, three, and six. I want this rig back in the air." He added, his voice low and steady, "Do not let my ship sink into a swamp of garbage."

Zix nodded quickly. "Yes, Admiral. We'll get her in the air." He peered out the window at the oil surrounding their floating train. "She's got a tight seal. The *Endeavor*'s not going to sink."

The cabin door opened and a dragonfly flew into the room. "We'll have lift thrusters back online in three minutes," she reported.

A clattering noise sounded against the *Endeavor*'s hull, making Jed jump. He peered out of a window and saw the dread closing in once again. Hundreds of them still stood on the riverbanks, launching their grappling hooks at the floundering ship. The lucky few who had managed to stay aboard and survive the *Endeavor*'s crash landing were pounding on the outsides of the boxcar again.

"We don't have three minutes," Lyle said. "We don't even have one."

The ceiling snapped above them. A sliver of light appeared as a patchwork piece of bulkhead was pried open. Dread fingers poked through the slit.

"Do the rear thrusters work?" Jed asked.

Lyle gave him a dismissive look. "We need to go up, not straight ahead."

"We can ride the river until the dragonflies fix the lift thrusters."

"Maybe he's right," Zix said. "My dragonflies sealed this ship up tight. We might have a few leaks, but nothing that's going to drown her."

"Punching the rear thrusters could send us nosediving into the river," Lyle said.

The bulkhead panel above them ripped away another few inches. The dread continued pulling, slipping their arms through and trying to grab someone—anyone—below. They laughed maniacally at each groan and squeal of the ship's framing as they pulled it away.

"We need to move," Jed said, ducking. "If we wait for the lift thrusters, we're going to die."

Lyle turned to Zix. "Do it."

Zix yanked a lever and a whoosh erupted behind them. The *Endeavor* shot forward, flinging off the dread. They continued straight, even though the river veered sharply left. Zix twisted another lever, and the *Endeavor* responded. The oil's current helped direct their makeshift boat forward as Zix worked the controls with lightning speed.

"One problem with your plan," Lyle said to Jed. "This river empties off the edge of the barge. We'll be free-falling in less than a mile."

With Lyle's words, Zix's retractable eyes extended slightly, as if focusing extra intensely. He pulled levers and pushed buttons, and the lift thrusters sputtered, jostling the ship from side to side as they tried unsuccessfully to again lift the train into the air. One of Zix's hose-shaped eyes swiveled, glancing at a gauge on the control panel. The gauge had an electricity symbol underneath a dial, and the red needle on the gauge was rising slowly toward the 50 percent mark.

Jed peered out the window of the train again. In the darkness ahead, he could see the edge of the barge. A great wall of dark smoke. *The fog.*

He squinted at the boundary. "I don't see a cliff," he said. "Are you sure it's there?"

Lyle and Zix looked at each other, but neither answered Jed.

Faster and faster they sped toward the wall of fog.

"Five percent more and I can engage lift thrusters," Zix said, watching the needle crawl from forty-five to forty-six percent. "We just need a little more time."

Forty-seven percent.

"Come on," Lyle said, his voice pleading with the energy gauge. "Come on."

Forty-eight percent.

A loud snap echoed from the back of the train. Engines whined, and steam hissed from a series of pipes along the walls. The needle on the energy gauge plummeted from 49 percent to 15 percent, where it remained steady.

"N-n-no . . ." Zix stammered. The vivid green light from his eyes dimmed, as if his own energy supply had drained instead of the ship's. "No."

"What happened?" Lyle demanded.

"One of the ion batteries ruptured under the stress."

"Isn't there something you can do?" Jed asked.

Zix slowly shook his head. "Give me three days and a half dozen junk runs, maybe."

"Can't we stop the train?" Jed asked.

"All we have operational are the rear thrusters," Zix said. "The *Endeavor* weighs nearly two thousand tons. That's four million pounds. There's no stopping her." He sighed in defeat, slumping down in his chair. Sirens squawked and warning lights flashed, but Zix was no longer pulling levers or pushing buttons at the control panel.

The train sped forward, unstoppable, toward the edge of the barge, and then they punched into the fog.

Jed

The *Endeavor* shot off the edge of the barge and through the wall of fog. A bright orange sky lit the world ahead.

The river of oil was no longer beneath them. In fact, *nothing* was beneath them—only open air and a distant, blurred pile of junk.

The energy gauge dropped to 0 percent. For a moment, the ship hung motionless in the air. Zix clicked the starter, but there was no response. "There's nothing I can do," he said.

Jed's stomach felt like overcooked noodles.

Then the train began to fall.

The spark of an idea popped to life in Jed's mind. It was crazy, but crazy things seem a lot less crazy when the other option is smashing a flying train into a giant junkyard. "Keep trying," he said to Zix before rushing from the cabin.

"Where are you going?" Lyle called after him.

As Jed bolted toward the engine room, the corridor began to tilt under him. The train was in a free fall. The ship rolled in the air, and then Jed was running on walls instead of floor. Soon, he reached the door to the garden cabin and flung it open.

The train tilted upward in its spin. The door at the end of the corridor was now directly *up*. The train car was vertical. Lemons and peaches fell from their trees, pelting him. Jed climbed as quickly as possible, using the trees for grip. He realized with a sudden sickness that there was no way he would make it in time. Not at this pace, anyway.

"Come on," he said to the train. "Just turn the other way."

Slowly, the train continued to rotate end over end, until, as he'd hoped, up was now down.

The cabin door he needed was right below him. He released his grip on the branch he was holding and fell toward it, the impact of his landing jolting through him. He pried open the door at his feet and stared at the greenhouse cabin—straight down from where he stood. Plants and soil showered the corridor.

Sucking in a breath, he dropped into the opening and fell the entire length of the greenhouse. Once again, he crashed into the next door, crumpling into a heap from the pain of the impact. The loose soil barely softened the landing.

One more cabin, he told himself.

He opened the door at his feet and jumped.

Soaring through the mess hall, he landed hard for the third time, but when he opened this door, he saw it—the ion engine.

As Zix had suspected, the ion battery had blown its circuits. Their charred remnants clattered around the engine core in dead, blackened chunks. They'd blown away from the copper lines that now dribbled with sparks.

"This better work," he said aloud, sucking in a nervous breath.

Jed dropped to the engine core, pulling off his shirt and exposing his golden gears and golden keyhole. He remembered the searing heat inside himself in the iron forest, but he didn't hesitate, grabbing both copper lines and plugging their bare ends into the hole in his chest.

Jed's body shuddered as the ship drank his energy.

Lights flickered.

His vision wobbled and darkened.

But then, the deep growl of the engine core hummed back to life.

Jed's legs were weak, and he could barely stand. The thirsty engine depleted his energy until he was too dizzy to think. He tipped forward on the engine room floor and collapsed.

Jed

Jed stood on a flat green hilltop under a bright blue sky. Fields of lush grass surrounded the view, and at his feet, heaps of diamonds sparkled in the radiant sunlight. They sat in mounds, like piled snowdrifts, brilliant rainbow flashes of color glinting in their depths. He stared transfixed, and then he picked one up. Its crystalline shape bent the sunlight, sending bright sparks of light outward.

"Where am I?"

He thought of the *Endeavor* plummeting through the air, and he remembered plugging the wires into his chest. *I'm dead*, he thought. *Or I'm dreaming.* But it felt like he belonged here, wherever here was. *Or I'm home.*

A black shape emerged on the horizon. It wobbled as it

drew closer. Dark smoke chugged from its exhaust valves, staining the perfect blue sky with oily clouds. It creaked and squealed as its insect legs dragged it closer. Jaws opened. A shriek pierced the air.

It wants the diamonds, he realized. *No. They're mine.*

Another shriek shot toward Jed.

"No!" Jed yelled. "Go away!"

It continued forward.

"Get away!" Jed yelled again.

Stomp.

Stomp.

Stomp.

Heat burned inside Jed. He stretched out a hand. "No!" he shouted. A bolt of power shot from Jed, knocking the creature down the hill.

Jed sprang up, his eyes wide open. He wasn't on the hilltop or the engine room anymore. He was in the med box, back in the *Endeavor*, his chest throbbing with pain.

Something crashed against the far wall.

Lyle.

He'd slammed into a set of supply shelves.

"What's going on?" Jed asked. "Are you okay?"

Lyle stood and stumbled in the mess of medical supplies at his feet.

The med box door opened. Zix peeked in, his eyes swiveling in two different directions. One eye found Lyle and the other found Jed. "What happened?" he asked.

"Nothing," Lyle said. "Everything's fine. Go back to your post."

"But—" Zix began.

"Now," Lyle snapped.

Zix nodded and left. "Aye, sir."

Jed stared at Lyle. "So, what *did* happen?"

Lyle cleared his throat. "You plugged yourself into the ion battery. You saved the ship, but you took some pretty bad burns to your chest."

"It worked?"

Lyle nodded. "You're lucky you're not dead. That battery could have melted your gears into a pile of clunk."

"I figured we were going to die anyway, so taking the risk didn't really matter, right?" Jed shrugged.

"Well, you'll need a bit of medical care, but you should be all right."

Jed glanced at the mess of supplies on the floor and the broken shelf on the wall. "How did you end up over there? You know, on the floor. Covered in scrap."

Lyle cleared his throat again. "I was making sure you were okay after the incident with the battery, and . . . something happened."

"Something happened?"

"It was probably due to the fact that you plugged yourself into a ship's engine core."

Lyle's voice sounded off, but Jed couldn't pinpoint why.

"But you flew across the room."

"Yes."

"And that doesn't seem a tiny bit weird to you?"

"I told you, you were built with incredible powers. When I was checking on you, your body reacted."

"Okay."

"You should get some rest," Lyle said.

"I'm not really tired. Just hungry."

Lyle nodded. "I'll have Alice check your wounds. If everything looks okay, you can join me in the kitchen."

Jed thought for a moment as he looked at Lyle. "You built her, right?" Jed asked. "Alice, I mean."

Lyle nodded. "I built all of the dragonflies. You know that."

"Then why don't her legs work? Can't you fix them?"

"Some wounds can be fixed. Some can't. You might have noticed; she's a lot more gears and scrap than many of the others on this train. When I found her body, she'd suffered a terrible death. I performed what repairs I could, but there's only so much a gearsmith can do. I did bring her back to life after all. Even though there wasn't much left of her."

Jed nodded. "I know. I just wish there was something you could do."

Lyle rested a hand on Jed's shoulder. "Rest. Alice will be around if you need anything."

. . .

Alice cringed as she pulled away the bandaging. "I'm sorry. Did that hurt?"

Jed shook his head, wincing. "No. It's not you. It just hurts all over."

"This should help." Alice held up a small vial in her free hand. "Aloe. It might sting a bit, but I promise it will help." She tipped the bottle, and cool droplets splashed onto his blistered skin. "That was incredibly stupid, you know," she said. "Plugging yourself into the ship."

"Thanks?"

"Anytime."

Jed tried not to move as the oil spread across his wounds.

Alice replaced the old bandage with a new one. "Is it helping?" she asked.

"I think so."

"Good. Because we're going to need you."

"For what?"

"That's classified."

Her metal face drew into a kind smile before she turned and left the room. Jed was alone once again, listening to the soft hum of the *Endeavor*'s ion engine. Thoughts of Shay and Ryan drifted through his mind. Were they still looking for him? He closed his eyes and pictured them. As he did, his mind felt like it was stretching beyond his head. It stretched further and further like a giant bubble. Dull images flickered through his eyes as if they weren't shut at all. The longer he focused on Shay, the more her consciousness bonded with his own until he was once again inside her head.

Shay

The scritchmice dragged Shay and Ryan from the deck of the small shuttlenought onto the gangplank now docked against the massive dreadnought of Captain Swillface Clunkrucket.

"Hope yer ready to get boiled, Princess," the leader scritch said with a sneer.

Shay nodded once. "Quite ready."

The dread marched them across to the dreadnought's deck. Mobs of dread eyed them as they walked. Ryan chewed on his bottom lip, but Shay wasn't afraid of a bunch of scritchwhelps. Whoever this Clunkrucket was, he probably thought he was the ickiest, scariest, meanest, biggest, rottenest, scoundreliest, scritchiest scritchmutt in all of Scritcherdom.

"I hope you know what you're doing," Ryan mumbled to her.

"Nope. No idea," Shay said.

Ryan's face went blank. "Um . . . oh."

The dread pushed them forward toward the captain's quarters. Two guards stood at the entrance.

"Got a little snack for the captain," the dread leader said.

The guards exchanged smiles, then nodded for them to proceed.

They opened the door, and standing before them was the ickiest, scariest, meanest, biggest, rottenest, scoundreliest, scritchiest scritchmutt in all of Scritcherdom.

"Ugly Mouse!" Shay screeched, wriggling free from the ropes that Fumbly Mouse *still* hadn't gotten right.

Captain Bog's mouth opened. "Shay?" he said, his voice wavering.

She rushed into the room and plowed into him, wrapping her arms around his barrel chest. "Yep. It's me!"

Captain Bog grinned at her. "I can't believe it's you," he said, shaking his head. "How did you find me?" He looked around the room. "Is Jed with you?"

Shay shook her head. "Jed broke. Just a little." She held up her thumb and index finger a half an inch apart from each other to show just how little. "But then he ran away, and now he's lost."

"He's alive though?"

"Yep. Alive and broken," she said cheerily.

Bog looked past Shay and squinted at Ryan. "I know you

from somewhere." Before Ryan could respond, Bog tapped a finger in the air at him. "Ah yes. The etchings we posted in every township for thirty sunfalls. You're—"

"Ryan."

Bog nodded, as if now recalling the name. "It seems you folks have got a bit of a wandering problem. First you and Mary mosey off to who-the-clunk-knows-where, and now Jed's gone, too? One of you really should buy a compass. Or maybe all of you. Or how about you just hold hands whenever you leave the house. Or all the time."

"Yeah. I get it," Ryan said, irritation in his tone.

Bog smirked.

"How about we change subjects?" Ryan said. "For starters, what in sun-roasted-slug-clunk is happening here on the barge?"

Bog's smirk widened. "Ah. You must be referring to my little campaign."

"Campaign?"

"The No-More-Traitorous-Dread-King campaign I started. It's quite popular."

"And by 'popular,' you mean 'a full-scale war'?"

Bog shrugged. "Not bad for three weeks' work, eh?"

"I'll say," Shay said approvingly.

"These clunkheads are easier to manipulate than a wad of slug snot," Bog said. He picked up an empty can of creamed corn from the ground and chucked it at one of the dread standing guard. The can bounced off the head of the guard, who straightened his spine and saluted Bog.

"Aye, sir?"

"At ease, you gnarled knot of scrap. Oh, and did you know you look like a washing machine that got stepped on by a house?"

"Yes, sir!" the dread said, saluting again.

Bog just rolled his eyes. "See what I mean? It doesn't exactly take the intellect of an airship engineer to get these bolt-brained maggots to do what you want."

"How much of the dread fleet do you control?" Ryan asked.

"As of today? About seventy-five thousand. But"—he shrugged—"they'll switch allegiances at the drop of a hook. Can't trust the bunch of ugly buggers." Bog motioned to the dread guards. "Go patrol the hallways or something."

The dreads nodded and walked out of the room, shutting the door after them.

Once they were gone, Bog turned to Ryan. "To be honest, they'll probably only follow me until I help them shoot down their former dread king. Whenever they question my authority I just remind them of the traitorous clunk-bucket we're hunting, and they seem to forget that I don't actually *have* any real authority. Scrap-brained slug lickers." He sighed. "So, what's your story, then?" he asked Ryan. "Where were you all that time we were posting etchings of your pretty mug around the yard?"

"I was stowed away on Lyle's ship. I hid there in case Lyle found Jed."

"Lyle? You mean the *former* dread king?"

Ryan nodded. "Long story short, after Jed showed up, Shay and I ended up on a life raft."

"Not before blasting my ship to scrap," Bog said.

"Lyle was trying to shoot *us* down. Not you," Ryan said.

"You best not tell my dread that," Bog said. "I've built my whole crusade on the assumption that their dread king was a filthy traitor who shoots down his own dreadnoughts."

"So, now you're the new king of the dread?" Ryan asked.

"That's right. Captain Swillface Clunkrucket at your service." He tipped an imaginary hat. "At least as long as I'm hunting Lyle."

"Then we need your help," Ryan said. "I believe Lyle is still looking for Jed. We need to find him before Lyle does."

Bog's brow furrowed. "What's Lyle want him for?"

"Because he built him, silly," Shay said as if it was obvious.

Bog's mouth opened slowly. "Excuse me? Did you just say, 'built him'? And by 'him,' you mean Jed?"

"We have a few things to explain," Ryan said.

Jed

Lyle's kitchen smelled like fresh basil and hand-kneaded bread. Jed stirred a small pot of tomato sauce as Lyle stretched a disk of dough.

"Do you know why I brought you here?" Lyle asked.

Jed began grating a block of mozzarella cheese into a bowl. "To make pizza?"

Lyle smiled. "Not to my kitchen. To the *Endeavor*."

"Something about training me to save the world?"

Lyle tossed his disk of dough into the air. It spun, stretching wider. He expertly caught the dough and then spun it in the air again. He paused for a moment and gave Jed a serious look. "I made a mistake with the dread."

Jed laughed. "You *think* so? What gave you that idea?"

Lyle glared at Jed. "I don't need a reminder. When I made them originally, I thought I could use them for good."

Jed almost laughed again. How could anyone think those things could ever be used for something good?

Lyle continued. "But they're out of control now, and they must be stopped. So many of them have turned against me that I can't do it on my own. I need your help, or innocent people are going to die."

"Innocent people are probably already dying."

"Even more of a reason to help me, then."

"What am I supposed to do about that? If you remember, they don't exactly listen to me. They pretty much just want to eat me alive."

"Limitless power is locked inside of you, Jed. All you need is the right key to unlock it." He set down the dough and walked over to Jed. Reaching into his pocket, he pulled out a black key.

"What's that?"

He pointed to Jed's chest. "The first step to unlocking your powers."

"What powers?"

"The kind of powers Alice saw you use in the forest. But those were only the beginning." Key raised, he stepped toward Jed. Instinctively, Jed stumbled backward. Lyle cocked his head. He motioned to the key. "It's just a piece of metal. It's not going to hurt you. Like I said . . . this will unlock your true potential. It's the only way."

Lyle stepped forward again, but something inside Jed's chest made him want to vomit. It felt like black sludge dripping down his throat into his stomach. The key felt like a serpent—its eyes on Jed's, ready and waiting to strike. He shook his head. "No."

"No?"

"Something's wrong with that key. I—I don't know what it is. Maybe a memory? It just feels . . . *wrong*. It's . . . it's all wrong."

"But you don't have any memories."

"You don't know that," Jed snapped. "I can remember *some* things. I just don't know what. They're more like feelings. And they're telling me that key is going to hurt me."

Lyle shook his head. "It's not going to hurt you. I promise."

"No," Jed said firmly. Another feeling surfaced inside him as he stared at the key. It was the same feeling he'd had during the dream. "That's what you were doing before," he said. "In the med box. You were trying to use that key on me. Weren't you?"

Lyle shifted uncomfortably. "Yes." He cleared his throat. "I'm sorry for that," he said. "I should have waited for you to wake up. I just wanted to fix you. That's what this key will do. Everything you forgot—all of your memories—will return in an instant if you use this key."

"My memories?" Jed asked.

Lyle nodded. "Everything you've forgotten. Back"—he snapped his fingers—"like *that*."

Jed reached out to touch the key, but the sick feeling returned. This time it hit him with a force that made him wretch. There was something deeply *wrong* with that key. He paused, hand still reaching for it.

"Is there a problem?" Lyle asked.

Jed's hand dropped to his side. "There has to be another way to access my powers. Otherwise, how would I have done what I did in the iron forest?"

"Alice told me how dangerous that was for you. Your powers were unstable. Erratic. But this key will ensure that you can control them perfectly. Quick as a spark."

A voice surfaced in Jed's mind. A memory someone once told him. "Quick fixes don't last," Jed said out loud. "You want something to work right, it's going to take the right kind of work."

Lyle gave him an amused look. "Did you read that in a book of quotes?"

Jed met his eyes. He couldn't remember *who* had told him that. Something inside him whispered that it was his father who'd said it, but that didn't make sense, because Lyle was supposedly his father.

Lyle returned the key to his pocket. "Fine. You want me to teach you? I can teach you. But while you're wasting time trying to learn something that you could have access to right at this moment, people are going to die. Are you sure that's what you want?"

"Maybe I'll learn faster than you think."

"And maybe you won't."

"I guess we'll see, then, won't we?"

Lyle leaned closer. "It's not going to be a stroll through the clouds. Unlocking what's inside of you on your own is going to hurt."

"I'm not afraid of pain."

"Not yet. But before this is over, you'll ask me for the key."

Jed stood up straighter. "We'll see."

Lyle nodded several times too many. "Then I suppose we should get started. Follow me." He stood and motioned Jed toward a heavily locked door in the kitchen. Lyle placed his palm in the very center of the door's thick steel and waited.

Lock after lock began to unlatch until the door hissed and relaxed open. Amber light glowed from the open seal. Lyle entered, and Jed followed.

The cabin's walls were lined with cabinets and drawers. In front of the cabinets on the west wall there were three waist-high pedestals. Each pedestal held a single, sparkling diamond—exactly like the diamonds he'd seen in his dream. Each shimmering jewel was smaller than a pea and each a different color.

The east wall had a small alcove in its center where a mechanical suit hung anchored in place. The suit had only one arm and a torso. It was an intricate skeletal cage made from the same golden metal inside of Jed.

The two walls looked like opposites: the tiny, simple diamonds across from the huge mechanical suit.

Lyle walked to a yellow diamond on one of the pedestals and picked it up. He held it for Jed to see. "This is called a life spark," he said. "Every gold has one. It's what gives us life."

"Every gold? You mean, there's more like me?"

"A whole city," Lyle said.

"Where?"

"Another story for another day," Lyle said. Jed wanted to press him for more details, but Lyle continued before he could say anything else. "Like I said before, each gold has a life spark. You and I are machines. But what separates us from a garbage disposal or a microwave is one of these." He held up the life spark.

"So it's like a brain?"

Lyle considered the idea. "You could think of it like that. A human without a brain is nothing more than skin, bones, and blood. A gold without a spark is nothing more than gears, batteries, and gold. Never forget: We are no less alive than they are. Don't ever let them convince you otherwise."

"Where did you get these sparks?"

"I used to be a gold gearsmith. It was my job to research and modify life sparks. These were collected from golds who didn't need them anymore."

"You mean you took them from dead bodies?"

"I suppose you could say it like that."

"So . . . you're like a zombie?

"What?"

"You collected brains from dead golds. That kind of sounds like a zombie to me."

Lyle sighed. "That's not important. What *is* important, is that I discovered a way not only to reactivate dead sparks, but also to *modify* them."

"What about your dragonflies? Do they have sparks? And what about the dread?"

"They have fragments of sparks."

"Fragments? What do you mean?"

"Sparks aren't easy to come by. I didn't have an endless supply to work with. So . . . I carefully shattered some of the sparks into little pieces and used the fragments to bring the human bodies back to life."

"*Back* to life?" Jed asked. "They all used to be dead humans?"

"Yes. I rebuilt their bodies with metal, then rebuilt their souls with shattered life sparks. My dragonflies are . . . shall we say . . . an upgraded model? They each have nearly a tenth of a spark instead of the thousandth that a dread has."

A memory of a book he'd once read popped into Jed's mind. "So, you're not a zombie after all. You're that doctor who built Frankenstein. Or was the doctor's name Frankenstein? I can't remember."

"Anyway . . ." Lyle said, ignoring the comment, "sparks can interact with junk. I tapped into that power, creating modifications. I've managed to modulate some life sparks with special abilities." He led Jed to the other two pedestals. "This one," he said, picking up the red spark and twisting it in the light, "is called mutiny. And that one," he said pointing to the blue spark still on its pedestal, "is called rally. All of the powers inside of you are based on a combination of mutiny and rally."

"What do they do?" Jed asked.

Lyle opened a drawer in the wall that was full of junk: an old sneaker, an empty grocery bag, a small telescope, and a book. He pulled out the drawer and emptied the contents onto the floor. He then pinched the blue spark and walked to the mechanical suit on the wall. Carefully, he set the spark in the center of the suit's right palm. A hum vibrated the cabin and the arm glowed a dull blue. Lyle turned his back to the suit and lifted his arm.

The suit began to move. It weaved itself around Lyle's right arm and upper body wrapping him in a tight cocoon. His left arm was free, but his mechanically tethered right arm now held the spark and pulsed with blue light.

He lifted the glowing arm and aimed it at the pile of junk. He then flipped a switch on the suit with his free hand. The hum deepened, and the glow brightened. The junk began to wobble on the floor then leaped up and stuck onto the end of the suit's arm.

Lyle flipped the switch off. The hum died, and the junk fell into a pile once again.

"That was the rally spark," he said.

"So it's like a magnet?" Jed asked. "But anything sticks to it?"

"With enough battery power, yes. This spark on its own isn't strong enough to attract sizable items. That's why it didn't rip the train's floor out from under us."

Jed hadn't considered that. "Oh."

"But string multiple blue sparks together and give them enough battery power, and you could pull anything you want. Also, the effect happens both ways, meaning: Try to pull something bigger than you, and you'll be the one who gets pulled."

"What does the other spark do?"

Lyle used his untethered left arm to remove the blue

diamond and replace it with the red one. Once again, the arm glowed—this time red. He aimed it at the pile of junk and flipped the switch. Crimson light glowed through the gaps in the suit and the pieces flew away from him as if a sudden gust of wind had just slammed into them.

"Like an upside-down magnet," Jed said.

"Yes."

Jed looked at his own hands. "Do I have those inside me?" He asked. "The mutiny and rally sparks?"

"I'd say you have a few inside of you; ninety-four thousand or so."

Jed stared at Lyle, stunned. "Are you being serious?"

"Ninety-four thousand one hundred and twenty-eight. My engineers and I worked for years modifying each one of them until we ended up with roughly thirty-one thousand of each type."

"I don't understand," Jed said. "Where did you get that many sparks?"

Lyle smiled. "You said it yourself. I'm Frankenstein. And you are my greatest creation."

Jed

Alice rousted Jed from his bed early the next morning and ushered him down the length of the train, headed toward the rear car. Dragonflies squeezed past them, bustling to and fro with their arms full of scrap. Jed watched them go and wondered. Alice intercepted his curious look and answered it.

"The admiral had us convert his workshop into a training box for you," she said.

"A training box?"

"Yes, and you'd better appreciate it," she said. "We were up all night."

"I'd ask more questions," Jed said, "but you'd just tell me everything was classified."

Alice smiled. "You might actually be a quick learner," she

said, echoing Jed's own words. The affection in her voice made him walk a little taller.

Alice led him to the back of Lyle's cabin, through the kitchen, and back into the spark cabin. Everywhere she flew, she struggled to navigate the space. Jed figured it must be exhausting for her to live on a train and not be able to walk.

At the south end of the spark cabin, there was a new door smelling of freshly cut cedar. Alice opened it and motioned for Jed to enter. The once–workshop cabin now showed outlines where built-in cabinets had been removed, and a newly laid wooden floor creaked as Jed stepped onto it.

At the far end of the cabin, a large window let in a stunning amount of light. This was the rear of the train. Jed touched the glass and stared, captivated, by the beauty of the junkyard. A memory came to him—a small town with a salvage yard. The rusted, dirty contents of the yard from his memory looked angry and menacing. But this place . . . this junkyard was nothing like that. The sun gleamed over the piles with a soft amber radiance that made everything look a little like gold.

"I see you found your way here," Lyle said from behind him.

Jed turned around.

"A terrible sight, isn't it?" Lyle continued, shaking his head at the junkyard. "How often I wish I could get away from it all to find a place without junk."

"Alice said this was a training box?" Jed said.

"Of sorts. I wasn't anticipating training you when a simple turn of the key could fix all of that. . . ."

Jed gave him a flat look.

Lyle sighed. "Very well." He reached into his pocket and held up a small marble. "This is your first task," he said.

Jed gave the marble a skeptical look, and then several metal plates wired to the ceiling caught his attention. Each plate was no bigger than a sand dollar. He stared at them for a moment, wondering. Why did it seem like there were only questions and no answers?

"What am I supposed to do with a marble?" Jed asked, returning his attention to Lyle.

"If you want to save the world, you have to save yourself," Lyle answered simply. He stepped out of the room, closed the door, and locked it behind him with an audible click. Almost immediately, the metal plates on the ceiling opened and marbles—streams of them—rained down on Jed.

"Hey!" Jed yelled, ducking and covering his head with his hands as a colorful rain of marbles bounced off him. "What is this?"

"Find a way to stop it," Lyle said through the door, his voice muffled. "Or I can stop it with my key. It's your choice."

Jed gritted his teeth, sliding clumsily over the rolling, shifting layer of marbles that was quickly covering the floor of the car until he was safely standing in a corner. He wished Lyle would just drop the subject of the key, but now, with falling marbles drowning out thought and conversation, he figured it wouldn't be the best time to discuss the matter.

The noise didn't stop him from yelling one final complaint, though. "I don't think greatest creations should be buried in marbles!" Jed lost his balance, pitched forward, and caught himself against the wall. The marbles had piled up to his ankles. The recollection of ball pits—they were filled with colorful plastic balls and smelled like French fries—threatened to derail Jed's focus.

"Now is not the time," he said through gritted teeth. "Think."

The marbles thundered down, inching up to his knees. The rally spark would call all the marbles in the car to him. Not good. His other option was mutiny—pushing the marbles back to where they came from. Smarter.

If only he knew how to do that.

Jed tried to recall his experience in the forest. He focused on a big blue marble in the growing sea of marbles and concentrated.

"Move," he said. The marble did move . . . as another hundred marbles buried it deeper beneath them. The marbles went up to his waist now, the weight squishing down on his toes.

"Move!" he shouted at the now-vanished blue orb. More marbles buried it further.

Jed searched again for the warmth—the heat—he had once felt, but now he couldn't find it. Maybe the thundering downpour of marbles had something to do with it.

I know what the mutiny spark feels like, he thought. *It's like . . . warm metal. And when it was turned on, I was connected to everything around me just for a second. But now it's off. Am I just supposed to be able to flip a switch or something? What kind of training is this?*

"Hey!" Jed shouted at the door. Lyle had vanished entirely.

Jed was alone, and the marbles were piling up higher. They bounced off his shoulders and landed near where his elbows were rapidly disappearing. It was getting harder and harder to move his arms. He'd have to start treading marbles soon.

"Move! Move! Move!" he yelled again and again. The marbles kept coming down.

Starting to panic, Jed felt a word pop into his mind: SPLAGHETTI. That word again. Jed closed his eyes and dug into himself.

The heat inside him began to light up. Each time a marble twanged off his ear or bounced against his forehead, the more urgently he fanned the tiny, growing spark. If he didn't do this ... well, he'd probably be the first person—or *gold* not-person—to experience death by marbles.

"Move!" he shouted again. Heat burst out of him and shot sideways. The marbles obeyed, blasting toward the ceiling in a giant mass. They crashed against the ceiling haphazardly. Some went back up through the trapdoors where marbles still rained down. Most fell right back to the bottom of the train car, though, pelting Jed like hail.

As quickly as it started, the marble rain stopped. Plexiglas on the back of the train car lifted two inches. The slush of marbles began an orange, red, green, and blue avalanche, dropping out of the train and down to the junkyard below. Jed slid across them until he was against the glass, too, giving him the perfect view of marbles pelting like shatterkegs to the ground. He tried to slow his breathing, but his heart still danced wildly in his chest.

Lyle opened the door.

"What was that?" Jed demanded. "Is that what you call training?"

"You used the spark, didn't you?" Lyle said. His voice didn't hold approval, but it also didn't sound upset. It sounded clinical.

"No thanks to you," Jed said, scrambling to his feet.

Lyle ignored his anger. "Would you like some lunch?" he asked. "I'm famished."

Jed

"What was with the marbles?" Jed demanded again. Lyle was working his way through an open-face avocado tartine, but for once, Jed didn't feel like eating. He wanted answers.

"Everyone I've ever known who achieved true greatness learned six characteristics: LEMONS. Letting go, endurance, movement, opportunity, unconcern, and suffering," Lyle said, his voice calm as he ignored Jed's question.

"*Unconcern* doesn't start with *n*," Jed said.

"No. It doesn't. That's the point. Don't concern yourself with what others tell you is right or wrong. Decide that for yourself. If you believe in your heart of hearts that a word starts with *n* despite everyone telling you otherwise, then you listen to *you*—not them. I'm not suggesting being stubborn or acting like a fool, I'm merely saying that it's okay to see the world differently from others.

"*L*. Letting go: Don't fixate on anything that weighs you down or keeps you from being the best you. If you're climbing a mountain while holding a bucket full of rocks, then let the rocks go.

"*E*. Endurance: That one's obvious.

"*M*. Movement: Everyone likes to plan, but not everyone likes to work.

"*O*. Opportunity: Learn to recognize it and act.

"Finally, *S*. Suffering: This may be the greatest tool of them all. Suffering builds strength. Minor suffering builds minor strength. Extreme suffering builds extreme strength. Embrace your wounds. They define you."

Jed scowled at that.

"You chose this," Lyle reminded him, finally acknowledging Jed's annoyance. "I offered a way out. One turn of my key and . . ."

"No thanks," Jed said, still frowning.

"The world depends on you getting this right," Lyle reminded him.

"And I did," Jed said. "Sort of," he amended.

"You used your mutiny spark once, and poorly," Lyle said. "Only my training—and yes, the marbles were part of that—can teach you to unleash its full power. Follow me."

Lyle patted his mouth with his napkin, folded it, and

placed it on the table. He stood and led Jed back into the spark cabin. Jed followed, but with distrust.

Lyle led Jed to a cabinet, opening it to reveal a jumble of keys.

"What are those for?" Jed asked.

"Take off your shirt," Lyle said.

Jed complied. The burn mark in the center of his chest had mostly healed. Fresh pink skin had grown over all but the small keyhole. He looked from the keyhole to the keys in the cabinets. "Do those belong to you?"

"Yes," Lyle said.

"What do they do?"

"Lots of things." He walked to one of the pedestals holding a spark. "A single spark contains the life and power of the gold. One spark is incredible, untapped potential."

"You told me all of this before," Jed said.

"A single spark can turn someone into a king in this world." He returned to the keys and thumbed through them until he found what he was looking for. Lifting a key from its hook, he turned to Jed and gestured to the hole in his chest. "May I?" he asked.

Apprehension swam in Jed's belly. He wanted to say no, but curiosity filled him. This key didn't frighten him like the black key did. He was . . . *unconcerned*.

Lyle step forward and put the key into Jed's chest. He turned it, and a small click echoed in the room.

A numbness trickled through Jed. He could no longer

feel the temperature of the room, the pressure of his feet on the ground, or even the bruises caused by falling marbles. He couldn't feel anything. It was as if the skin on his body had turned into a loose, soft bag. Jed shifted in place and realized that he was right. His skin sagged limply around his frame.

"Go ahead," Lyle said. "Step outside of your skin."

Instinctively, Jed put both hands into the hole in his chest and pulled himself free of his skin. Hidden underneath was a blinding body made entirely of sparks. They shimmered under the amber light of the cabin. Red, blue, and yellow—the sparks were woven through golden fibers and strands. For the first time, Jed saw himself. His true self. He was sparks and gold.

Who am I?

Outside of his skin, the world was just a photograph to Jed—one he couldn't touch or feel. Uncomfortable with the sensation and confused by the weirdness of it all, he stepped toward his discarded covering and wrapped it back around his body. "Fix it," he said to Lyle. "Make it part of me again."

Lyle turned around and rummaged through the keys. He lifted another one from its hook and slid it into Jed's chest. The key turned, and sensation rushed back into Jed as the skin tightened around his golden body.

"You need to decide right now," Lyle said. "You were built to change the world. I need to know your intentions. I can't have you throwing a fit every time something doesn't go your way."

Anger flared in Jed's throat. "How could I have known you

were going to bury me alive? That's not just something 'not going my way.'" He added huffily, "And I didn't throw a fit."

Lyle shrugged. "I can't tell you everything that I'm going to do, and I can't have you second-guessing me every time I try to teach you something. So, which is it: Are you in, or are you out?"

Jed stood there—arms folded—looking from Lyle to the door. Finally, he relaxed, letting his arms fall to his sides. He sighed once. "I'm in."

Jed

The training box smelled like electricity and child endangerment. Lyle wore his golden armor, the mutiny spark glowing with intimidation from his palm. Bins piled high with objects sat pushed against the walls behind him. Empty bins sat behind Jed.

"Good morning. The world is one day closer to ending today," Lyle said. "I don't say that to pressure you, but you must start progressing faster than you are."

"I'm trying," Jed said, wondering how those words weren't pressuring.

"Stop trying," Lyle said. He tossed a tiny metal bolt to the center of the room. "Pull the bolt toward you."

Jed reached out his hand as if to grab it. "Move . . ." he

whispered. "Come on . . . move." He searched deeper inside himself for the warmth. He tried to find the same spark he had activated the day before. He knew it was there, in him, but he had no idea how to find it.

"I—" he started but stopped himself before continuing. *No more excuses. No more whining. Figure it out, or don't.*

The corners of Lyle's mouth twitched just barely, as if delighted with Jed's choice not to whine. "There's a switch inside you—one that only you know how to activate. It's not something I can explain to you. It's something that you need to find."

"Move . . ." Jed said again to the bolt.

"Find your motivation. In the iron forest you thought you were being attacked. You activated the junk to survive. It seems to me that we need to replicate those circumstances."

Lyle activated his mutiny spark, motioned to the bin behind him, and sent debris flying toward Jed's face. Pens, rubber bands, a stapler, a small flashlight, and a hammer zoomed at him. Jed threw himself to the ground. The pieces of junk collided with the wooden wall.

"Are you trying to kill me?" Jed asked.

"Catch them with your rally spark," Lyle instructed. "Then put them in your bins. Keep them there with your mutiny spark." Any fatherly concern he'd ever shown was now gone. Lyle launched a box cutter, bag clips, a small statue, a wrench, and a Slinky toward Jed, who ducked. The box cutter zinged by, leaving the air ringing behind it.

"Use your sparks," Lyle commanded.

"I don't know how," Jed said, keeping one eye on Lyle and the other on the flying objects. Scissors zipped past his ear and stuck into the wall.

"You can," Lyle said. He sped up his pace, launching larger junk—wrenches, buckets, a lamp, wind-up teeth, and a drill—at Jed.

The shower of junk swirled around the room as Lyle emptied his bins and then used his mutiny spark to continue to fire on Jed. It was a mini-junkstorm in the cabin, with Lyle standing in the epicenter.

"Stop me," Lyle said.

Jed tried and failed. Even a simple penny became a much larger threat when zooming through the air at high speed, and the longer it took Jed to react, the faster Lyle made the pieces fly.

"The world won't stop while you figure out how to save it," Lyle taunted. "If you can't divide your attention between threats, you are destined to fail."

"I seriously question your teaching," Jed said, dodging a flock of thumbtacks.

"It's not my choice to do this," Lyle said, still sending junk shooting toward Jed. "You know the option I prefer."

"I'm not using that key," Jed exclaimed. "Stop bringing it up!"

"It's the only thing that will work," Lyle said. "You can't do this on your own. It's simply too—"

Heat rose in Jed's chest, and he waved a hand toward Lyle. A package of pencils, a broken plate, and a bicycle pedal reversed direction. The junkstorm spat back at Lyle. The heat in Jed's chest grew. More and more pieces fired at Lyle, reversing direction and swirling away from Jed.

"How . . ." Lyle began. He cut off his words and frowned. Anger boiled in his expression.

Jed felt the power inside of himself. It was a chain reaction, spark-to-spark, igniting like a fire. The junk in the room fell from the air and landed on the floor with a crash as his power met—and then overpowered—Lyle's.

Lyle swiped his suit-powered arms furiously, trying to counteract Jed's attempts, but it was no use.

Focusing intensely, Jed squinted and waved his hands at the fallen objects. The pieces began to gather in bunches, rolling across the floor like snowballs and collecting more junk. Balls of junk zipped back and forth over the floor, following Jed's command.

Once all the debris was collected, he directed the balls of helmets, dented pots, light fixtures, and empty deodorant containers to roll across the floor and hop into the bins behind him. When the floor was clear, Jed smiled proudly at Lyle.

"Well . . . done," Lyle said. But there was no true admiration in his tone. Instead, his voice sounded hollow. "That was unexpected."

Jed

Lyle left the training room without another word. Excitement hummed through Jed from his success. He'd done it. If even for just a moment, he'd controlled the sparks. He wanted to share what he'd done with someone, but Lyle had seemed less than enthusiastic about the accomplishment. Maybe he could tell Alice. No . . . she was flying security detail around the *Endeavor* until lunchtime. An odd loneliness stung him as he realized that the only other one he wanted to tell was an empty tin can of cherry pie filling.

He grabbed his red backpack and headed to the crew workshop cabin. Alone, he retrieved Sprocket from the backpack. "I beat him at his own game today," he said to her with a smile as he rummaged around the workshop for parts.

"He doesn't think I can do it on my own, but I proved him wrong." Jed found a handful of half-dollar-size washers. "I'm stronger than he thinks, and I don't need his scrap little key." Jed squeezed the washers onto the ends of Sprocket's legs. "Are those okay for feet?" he asked.

He then found some braided copper wire that he fastened to the end of the can for a long tail. "How does that feel?" he asked her.

A faint buzzing noise sounded from inside the can.

Jed froze, holding her in his lap.

Heat welled in his chest like it had before, but he wasn't activating the mutiny or rally sparks. This was something else. He closed his eyes. This was coming from the life sparks inside him. He could almost see them releasing their power.

"Gzzz . . ." Sprocket said.

Jed's heart jumped.

"Sprocket?" he said.

Nothing.

The workshop door was flung open, and Dak and Brindle entered.

"Hey, there," Brindle said. "Working on anything interesting?" He hovered over Jed and lifted an eyebrow at Sprocket. "Well that's *interesting*, I suppose. Dak and I are going to the library for some cards. Wanna join?"

Jed smiled. "Sure."

He stuffed Sprocket into his backpack and walked with them.

"We never properly thanked you for saving our skins back in the gulch," Brindle said.

Jed wasn't about to point out that most of the dragonflies didn't really have much skin.

Dak clapped him on the back and gave Jed a single nod. "Yeah. What he said."

"Alice said you plugged yourself into the ion battery," Brindle said. "That true?"

Jed nodded. "Looking back," he said, "it doesn't seem like the smartest idea."

"Well, it worked," Dak said. "And you're alive."

"Where have you been?" Brindle asked. "Haven't seen you around. Rumors spread the way rumors do when all's you got is a dozen cabins of living space to share. Heard Admiral locked you away or some such."

"Or some such," Jed said. "Lyle is *supposedly* training me."

"Training you for what?" Brindle asked. "A mission?"

"I guess," Jed said.

"A *secret* mission?" Dak asked as they entered the library.

Before Jed could respond, the *Endeavor* jolted. A siren blared. The wall comm crackled to life with Zix's voice. "All engine techs to their stations. Blown thermo induction valve. Pistons twenty-four through thirty-seven are off-line."

Dak and Brindle stood. "That's us," Brindle said, stuffing the deck of cards back into his pocket in frustration. "Always something breaking on this clunk heap. We needed a good four more days back in the gulch before we lifted her into the air."

"At *least* four," Dak said. "Could've used twice that."

"If we lose any more parts, we'll have to land in a township port," Brindle said.

A pop echoed through the cabin, and the comm crackled back to life. "We lost an ion capacitor," Zix said. "Navigation crews report to your stations and begin searching for the nearest township port."

"Slug clunk," Dak grunted.

"What's wrong with a township port?" Jed asked.

"They don't like our kind," Brindle said. "Coppers and irons see us as dread, and they'll smash us to scrap before you can say, 'Slug snot.'"

"They'll do the same to you if you aren't careful," Dak said, nodding to Jed's chest wound. "As soon as they know you got metal for muscle, they'll take turns using you for shatter practice."

The two dragonflies hurried from the library, headed for their stations.

Zix's voice crackled a third time on the wall comm. "Jed, report to the admiral's cabin for instruction."

Jed made his way to the back of the train toward Lyle's cabin. Lyle found him halfway there.

"What's going on?" Jed asked.

"Join me in town," Lyle said. "You're the only other one on board who won't draw attention." He fished around in his pocket and pulled out a handful of batteries. "Here," he said, handing the batteries to Jed. "These always make a port trip a bit better."

Jed pocketed the batteries, and he and Lyle made their way to the bridge, passing dragonflies who worked frantically on overtaxed engine parts.

"If you remember, we had to leave the gulch in a bit of a hurry," Lyle said. "The *Endeavor* wasn't quite ready for this long of a flight."

Zix met them on the bridge. He handed a paper to Lyle. "Here's the list of supplies we need if we want to stay in the air," he said.

The *Endeavor* limped through the air for nearly another hour, Lyle and Alice studying the maps and searching the skies for a township. Zix and the others hurried to and fro, patching breaks and trying to keep the ship together. Finally, Alice pointed to a distant black dot in the sky. "There's Lunkway," she said.

Jed plastered himself to a window, drinking in the view as Lunkway slowly came into his sight. The floating city sparked not-so-distant memories of another hovering, iceberg-shaped township. Needlelike buildings jutted up from the base of the small metropolis. *Spikes*, Jed remembered. Long rods extended from the underside of the township with propellers at their ends. More propellers than Jed could count spun in a blur to keep the township afloat.

"It's incredible," Jed said.

"Just be careful out there," Zix said. "We're not like them. If they see a single gear, you'll be blasted full of holes."

Lyle nodded. "Vile creatures, humans," he scowled.

The *Endeavor* circled Lunkway, looking for a port big enough for the massive train to land.

"There," Zix said, pointing to an open spot on the north side of the city.

"Is Lunkway a copper or an iron city?" Jed asked.

"Neither," Zix said. "It's a free-metal marketplace. All metals there."

"All metals except for gold," Lyle said.

. . .

It felt good to be on land. Jed took a few tentative steps forward. Tall, pointy buildings loomed over them, and people bustled through the streets, hurrying to and fro. There were more people crammed into just one street than Jed would have thought possible, and he wished he could talk to all of them. Find out their stories. Learn who they were.

You're not one of them, he thought. *They'll kill you if they know who you are.*

He stared at the happy faces, pleasantly chatting with one another as they walked, and he wondered if it were really true—if these strangers would hate him if they saw inside him.

As Lyle and Jed left the port and approached the city buildings, Jed noticed identical metal sheets posted by the doors on each structure. *Etchings* ... he remembered. They were announcements of some sort.

Lyle noticed them, too, and he approached the one closest to them. "Hmm," he muttered, reading the words pressed into the metal. "They've banded together."

"Who?" Jed asked.

"The irons and the coppers," he said. "Those metals can't even agree on what color the sky is, and now they're brothers in arms."

Jed leaned in closer and read the words himself.

JOIN THE I.C.C.A.D.
BE PART OF THE
IRON-COPPER COALITION AGAINST DREAD

Dread forces are engaged in civil war. Commanders of both iron and copper legions have signed a shatterpact for an unconditional ceasefire and a temporary alliance to launch a unified offensive against the dread.

This announcement will be etched across every township from Borenbunk to Farburrow. Everyone over the age of fourteen, clever or clunk-brained, is—as of this morning—officially invited into wartime service.

Report to Drockraven Outpost. Falcon transports run twenty-four-hour passage from every township.

"Isn't this a good thing?" Jed asked. "To have them all fighting the dread?"

Lyle shrugged. "Like Zix said, they won't see you, me, or any of the dragonflies as any different." He moved away, and Jed followed, glancing back at the signs one more time as they left.

Lyle took them from shop to shop, buying small, expensive parts for the *Endeavor*. He'd brought a cart full of batteries, which were slowly being swapped for engine parts. As they bartered with shopkeepers and edged around finagling junk wranglers, Jed began to wish they had more time to spend in the township. He liked being around the bustle of humans.

"Aren't you going to spend those batteries somewhere?" Lyle asked offhandedly, crossing another item off their list.

Jed had forgotten about the batteries in his pocket. "I don't know what to buy," he said.

Lyle nodded toward a shop called Trisky's Trinkets. "Why don't you try there?" He pointed to another gear shop across the street. "I'll be in here."

Jed walked to Trisky's Trinkets and opened the little glass door. Copper chimes clinked above his head as he entered.

"Welcome," a portly woman said. "Can I help you find anything?"

"Just looking around," Jed said.

"Well, let me know if you need any help."

Trinkets—piano keys and spoon wind chimes, light bulb wall hangings, mismatched boots decorated with marbles and chess pieces—were everywhere. Each new trinket he found made Jed smile all over again.

Jed turned the corner in the shop and spotted a glass jar with a copper dragonfly inside. The little dragonfly had intricately designed wings made from tiny bits of wire and metal. The wings were attached to a body made from a long, copper battery.

"Battery bugs," the shop owner said behind him.

"What?" Jed asked.

She shook the jar, but the lifeless dragonfly only bounced

around inside. "Hmm . . ." she said. "Looks like this one's got a dead battery. A charged bug will glow and flutter around. I'll give this to you for half price if you want."

Jed thought of Alice. He wanted to get her something for saving his life. At half price, he had just enough batteries. Maybe he could charge the bug and get it working again. "Okay," he said. "I'll take it."

She put the battery bug in a paper bag for Jed and thanked him for his business. He wanted to linger. He wanted to ask her about herself, to find out which trinket was her favorite . . . what she liked best about living in Lunkway . . . if she had a battery bug of her own.

You're not one of them, the voices said again. *They'll hate you if they know what you are. Go back to where it's safe. Go back to the* Endeavor.

He opened his mouth anyway to ask Trisky if she'd always lived in Lunkway. She looked up at him and smiled.

"Yes, dear?" she asked.

Jed shook his head. "Nothing. Sorry."

He walked out into the street and watched as people passed, suddenly feeling alone despite the crowds. He didn't belong here, but the *Endeavor* didn't feel like home either. Where did he belong? Jed stepped into a quiet alley off the main street to gather himself together. In the stillness, he dropped his backpack and leaned against a wall. He hung his head, thinking. A shuffle of motion inside his bag caught his eye. A strange noise followed.

Zzzort.

Jed froze. Was that a voice?

"Hello?" Jed said.

Zzzort!

Jed unzipped his bag and pulled out Sprocket. She stared at him with her rust-stained face and her bolts for eyes. "You're talking, aren't you? Because of me? Did I make you come alive?"

He suddenly felt incredibly foolish, standing in an alleyway talking to a can. He was probably going crazy.

"Crazzzy," Sprocket said.

Jed

O nce Lyle had traded his cartful of batteries for two cart-
fuls of supplies, they headed back to the *Endeavor*, each
pushing a heavy cart. As they walked the long dock to the
ship, Jed stared longingly at the township. Part of him wanted
to stay there and forget that a hundred thousand dread were
running loose in the junkyard. Even if Lyle helped him fully
develop his powers, Jed doubted he could stop them.

"When we're back in the air," Lyle said, "I want you to
meet me in the training box."

"So you can throw more junk at me? Sounds super fun."

Lyle sighed. "We're running out of time. My dragonflies
report that the dread fleet is still hunting us. They're going to

catch us if we just keep flying around in circles. Help unload the carts, then go to the training box. Immediately."

"Aye, aye, All-Powerful Admiral, sir." He gave Lyle a mock salute.

Lyle ignored him and stomped ahead.

Jed sighed. What if he just left the *Endeavor*? Looked for Shay and Ryan and Bog. They didn't seem like the monsters Lyle had made them out to be. But what if Lyle was right? What if they *were* after him? Maybe for his powers? Maybe for something else.

Jed met the crew inside the *Endeavor* and unloaded the carts. While the crew worked to get the train in the air, Jed replaced the dead battery in the battery bug he'd bought for Alice then found her in her cabin tinkering with one of the gears in her wings.

"Hey," he said.

She looked up and set down the screwdriver she'd been using.

"How was your little shopping trip?" she asked.

Jed shrugged. "Fine, I guess." He pulled the battery bug out of his pocket. Its green glow filled the cabin. "I got this for you. For, well, saving my life, I guess."

Alice's face softened from its usual hard-edged snark, and she gave him a genuine smile. "Thank you," she said, taking the battery bug from him, and studying the bright glow.

"I gotta meet Lyle for training, but ... thanks again," he said.

By the time he made his way to the training box, Lyle was already there.

The man set a wooden box on the floor.

"There's a bolt inside this box," he said to Jed. "I want you to rally it to yourself."

"I thought we already played the rally-the-bolt game," Jed said. "And, I sort of remember winning."

Lyle sneered. "Just because you got lucky once, doesn't mean a thing. If you can't perfectly control your sparks on command when shatterfire *isn't* being launched around you, how can you expect to do so in the middle of a war? Besides, this exercise is different. Your sparks are more powerful than you can imagine. They connect you to the junk—no matter how close, or how far away. Even if you can't see it."

"What does that mean?" Jed asked.

Lyle nudged the wooden box with his toe. Something rattled inside. "There's a metal bolt in this box. You can't see it, but it's there. I want you to close your eyes and use your sparks to connect with it. Let your sparks see it when your eyes can't. Once you link to it, rally it toward you."

Jed wanted to argue, but he remembered the strange sensation while in the iron forest. It was as if thousands of eyes all around were watching him. "I've felt that before," he said.

Lyle nodded and pointed to the box.

Jed stared at the box, trying to see through the surface.

"Close your eyes," Lyle said again. "Your sparks will be able to see it much, much better."

Jed tried, but he couldn't see anything.

"With my key," Lyle continued, "you will be connected to everything around you. Say you want a fresh egg, but there's none around. You'll be able to reach out with your sparks and find one—no matter how far away."

Jed thought back to when Lyle had taught him how to poach an egg. For the first time, Lyle's key felt just the tiniest bit tempting.

He shook his head. "I can do this on my own. I don't need that key."

"You can't," Lyle said, more bitter whisper than actual response.

Come on . . . Jed thought to himself. *Don't let Lyle be right*. . . .

He tried again, gently letting the heat warm through his sparks. Eyes closed, he could only see blackness. But after a few moments, he *could* sense something. Not the bolt, but a million different *somethings* around him. The connections deepened, and Jed began to feel lines linking him to everything.

"What's the problem?" Lyle asked, breaking Jed's concentration.

Jed opened his eyes. "I was . . . I was starting to see something."

Lyle shook his head. "Don't make things up just to impress me," he said. "The bolt hasn't moved. It's not working. If you can't move the bolt right now, I'm using the key."

"No!"

Lyle's teeth clamped together. "We don't have time for this. You either can, or you can't. And it looks like you can't. So we're done trying."

"We're not done trying," Jed said. He reached out his hand and felt for the bolt still inside the box. It was there. He *knew* it. Heat rushed through his sparks and something began to rattle inside the box. "I'm doing it!" Jed said, excitedly. "Look!"

Lyle looked nervously at the box. "Congratulations," he said dismissively. "You wiggled a bolt around inside a box. That's exactly what we need to win the war."

Angry heat welled inside of Jed. "I did what you said. I don't get it. It's like nothing I do is good enough. It's like you *want* me to fail."

"How about we see *just* how strong you think you are." Lyle studied Jed, then walked away. He left the box and shut the door behind him.

A light in the center of the ceiling flickered on above Jed. It was an odd yellow, almost amber color. It began to rotate. A siren began to blare.

"Hey, what's going on?" Jed called.

A clang echoed below him. The floor shuddered underneath his feet. Jed stared down as a sliver of white light appeared, running the length of the floor from one end of the box to the other—straight down its middle.

"Lyle?" Jed called again. "What's going on? Something's happening to the floor." No answer came from behind the closed door. "Lyle!" he shouted. His eyes flickered back and forth between the sliver of light and the door. Somewhere in the belly of the *Endeavor*, its guts began to grind, and the sliver of light widened.

Jed's heart raced.

The two halves of the floor were folding open away from each other underneath him, as if the box were a garbage chute emptying its cargo into the open sky.

The two halves of the floor continued to split, and the sliver of light grew wider. The angle steepened. Jed stumbled toward the center where the floor parted. Wisps of clouds rushed beneath him, blurring the junk below into a heap of brown and orange.

"Lyle!" he shouted. "Lyle, I'm going to fall!" His legs were split across the gap. A couple inches more and the floor would be too far apart for his feet to reach both sides.

The boxcar door opened. Lyle stood in the doorway, arms folded. "Do you still feel just as arrogant as you did a second ago?"

"Get me out of here!" Jed yelled.

"Get yourself out of there," Lyle said. "Rally your body to the training box's ceiling and you'll be just fine. Better yet, rally your body over here and join me for some cordon bleu. It's dinnertime."

"This isn't funny. I'm slipping." Jed's shoes could barely grip the unfolding panels anymore, they were so far apart.

"I'm not laughing," Lyle said. "Rallying a bolt isn't going to save the world. You're acting like a baby by not letting me unlock your true potential."

"Is that what this is about?" Jed said. "That key again?"

"If you want to win, you'll have to make sacrifices."

"That's not your choice. It's mine."

"But I'm the one standing next to the lever that holds your fate," Lyle said, a sinister tone to his voice.

"You can do whatever you want to me," Jed said, "but I'm not letting you touch me with that key."

Fury burned in Lyle's eyes. He gripped a lever by the doorway and pulled down hard. Jed's stomach clenched into a knot as the floor disappeared from underneath his feet. He didn't even have time to scream. He sucked in a half breath and waited to plummet from the *Endeavor*.

But he didn't fall. He stayed there, hovering.

Terror, relief, and confusion swelled inside him.

Clouds rushed past them over mountains of junk. And yet, Jed remained in place. "How?"

Lyle stared at him. He blinked. He stared again.

I'm doing it, Jed realized. *I'm rallying myself to the ceiling.*

And in that moment, Jed could feel it. The bond between him and the metal roof. That link was the only thing keeping him from falling into the sky. Jed reached for the link—that connection—and tugged.

His body shot up and slammed into the ceiling. He stuck to the panel of metal as if every inch of his skin was glued to it.

"Shut the doors," Jed yelled.

"No," Lyle said. He should have looked pleased at Jed's success, but he looked frustrated instead.

"Close them!"

Lyle cocked his head. "Why?"

"I passed your test."

"My test? This wasn't a test."

"Well, whatever it was—I passed. Now shut the doors so I can get down!"

"If you're as strong as you think," Lyle said, "then you can stay up there for much longer. Let's see how long."

"I don't want to. Shut the doors."

As Jed held his body to the ceiling, the heat he'd felt in the iron forest crept once again up his spine. It diffused through his body like molten metal. "I'm burning up," he said.

Lyle shook his head slightly, as though breaking whatever train of thought had kept him quiet.

Heat coursed through Jed. It was boiling him from the inside out. Jed closed his eyes. He slowed his breathing as much as he could while stuck dangling to the ceiling of an open train car.

He pulled in a deep breath and let it out just as slowly.

In . . . out.

In . . . out.

A recognition washed over him. He took more breaths, in and out, in and out. He saw something. A faucet . . . a valve . . . something. It connected his brain and his chest. Sparks inside him radiated with energy, leaking bits of power, heating his bones and gluing him to the top of the box. He reached for the valve and twisted. The valve shut off. The flow of energy stopped.

Jed's body peeled away from the ceiling and he began to fall out of the bottom of the train car.

He reached for the valve again and cranked it open. His

body slapped back up against the top of the box with a deafening thud. Pain and heat rippled through him. "That wasn't smart," he mumbled to himself.

His body throbbed, but to his surprise, Jed didn't want Lyle to shut the doors. He wanted the doors to stay open forever—to stay there in that moment forever. This feeling of power was unlike anything he had ever known.

It was exhilarating. He could control the flux valve.

Lyle reached for the lever to shut the doors.

"No!" Jed shouted. "Keep them open." The thrill, the rush overwhelmed Jed. He lowered himself slowly away from the ceiling and straightened his body until he was standing upright. He hovered in the middle of the boxcar and smiled at Lyle, thrilled by his breakthrough and expecting to see pride in Lyle's face.

Lyle stared back at him. Instead of pride, Jed saw something he hadn't seen before: jealousy. And in that look, Jed realized something critically important: Lyle wasn't on his side.

Jed's mind snapped to Shay and Ryan. Had *they* been on his side all this time?

He felt his vision begin to slip away and bond with Shay's until he could see through her eyes again.

Shay

"Hmm." Shay stroked her chin with extra-long thinking strokes. She studied the checkerboard and Captain Bog's black pieces.

He thinks he's so clever, doesn't he?

She gave the board a wicked grin, then lifted one of her red pieces and hopped over two of his little black ones.

"Ha-*ha!*" she said, picking up the pieces she'd just hopped over. "Bye-bye, little mouselet," she said to the first, before tossing it over her shoulder. "Bye-bye, little mouselet," she said to the second, tossing it over her other shoulder. "Two mouselets down. Seven to go."

Bog wasn't perturbed. He studied the board, nodding to himself. He looked *confident. Too* confident. Shay's gaze darted

147

back to the board. Her focus bounced from piece to piece, mouselet to mouselet, red to black.

And then she saw it.

The lurking mouselet.

It sat there, in the back, pretending not to be as dangerous as it was.

Maybe he hasn't seen it yet. Maybe he won't see it, she thought to herself.

She lifted her gaze to meet his. The captain's eyes were locked knowingly onto her own. A grin lifted the scars on his face. He looked down at the board—at the lurking mouselet.

"No," Shay said quickly. "Wait—wait—I want to take back my move."

Bog's head turned slowly to the left, then slowly to the right. He waggled his finger twice in the air. "Uh-uh-uh," he said. "No takebacks. You know the rules."

"But, but, *but*—"

But it was too late.

He scooped up the lurking black mouselet and began hopping over pieces.

Stomp.

Stomp.

Stomp.

Every stomp killed another defenseless red mouselet.

Five stomps.

Six stomps.

And then seven.

Nearly her entire army of mouselets lay dead on the board.

"Darlings!" she cried. "My little mouselets."

Bog nodded with delight in his eyes. One by one he picked up their lifeless corpses and stacked them into his hand. "Bye-bye, little mouselets." Bog chucked the handful over his shoulder.

Shay gave them a soft wave good-bye. "Farewell. You fought bravely."

"That they did," Bog said. "That they did."

Her last mouselet sat in the center of the board. Alone and afraid. Defenseless and whimpering. Mourning the loss of its fallen brothers and sisters. "Your move," Bog said. He leaned over the board and rested both elbows on the edge of the table.

Shay sat up straight and nodded stoically. If her lone mouselet was going to die, it was going to die fighting. She reached for the last of her pieces and lifted it high, ready to plunge it into the fray—to its inevitable demise.

Before she could set it down, something tickled the back of her brain. A whispery voice. No. It was more like shadowy eyes. Eyes stuck in her brain that weren't her own.

She looked up at Bog. He could see that there was something going on. "Shay? Are you all right?"

She smacked the side of her head a couple of times to jostle the eyes free. "Hmm," she said. "I think there are eyes in my head that aren't mine. Will you excuse me?"

She stood and began walking to the bathroom. "Go away," she whispered to the eyes. "Go find another mouse's brain to nibble on."

When she reached the bathroom, she locked the door and

turned around to study her face in the mirror. "Who are you?" she asked. "What do you want in my brain?"

. . .

Jed felt bits of himself returning, even though he stayed in Shay's vision.

"You can see me?" he asked.

Shay glared at the mirror. "I *knew* someone was in there," she said to herself. "Now, answer me. What sort of mouse are you?"

"Well," Jed began, "you've been calling me a broken mouse."

Shay's face lit up with excitement. "Really? That's you? You're alive?" She giggled and clapped her hands. "I knew it, I knew it, I knew it."

"What's going on?" Jed asked in her mind. "I don't know who you are."

"Of course, you do, silly," Shay said. "I'm Shay."

"Lyle said you kidnapped me."

Shay gasped. "Lyle? Are you with him?"

"Yes. I'm on his train."

Shay's eyes widened. "You're on the *Endeavor*? We're chasing that pesky squiggly boat. It's a very sneaky boat, isn't it?"

"I don't know what's going on," Jed said. "I can't remember anything."

Shay looked deeper into the mirror. "Lyle thought that might happen from that scary Awakening Key."

"What Awakening Key?"

"You put it in your chest and then *boom!*"

"What did it do to me?"

"Awakened your sparks," Shay said. "But Mouse King thought it might make your mind fuzzy. So he made a black key, too."

"Yes! He's been trying to use it on me. What does it do?"

"It's not a nice key at all," she said, shaking her head. "It deletes Jed and lets Lyle become new Jed."

Jed's stomach tightened. "New Jed?"

Shay nodded. "He wants your sparks, of course. So he can make things come alive like you can."

"I knew there was something wrong with that key," Jed said.

"You should get off of that squiggly boat," Shay said casually, "before he deletes you and steals all of your gold and sparks. That would be sad."

"How do I know if you're telling me the truth?"

Shay nodded to the mirror. "Clever mouse. Good for you. I might be a sneaky, conniving, wicked little clunk mouse! Right? Yes. Okay, behind the painting of a red tree, Mouse King keeps a secret box. Four, fourteen, nineteen. That's the secret. All of Mouse King's angry memories are inside. I used to sneak in there and watch them. Hmmm," she said, tapping her chin. "Watch fourteen–seventy-five. Then sixteen-sixteen. Then nineteen-three. And . . . oh, then thirty-three–eleven. That was an angry one. Watch them, then leave. Find somewhere safe. We will come for you."

Before Jed could respond, the vision had faded.

He was lying on his back in the center of the training box. The bay doors were closed, and Lyle stood looming over him. The man's hand was inside his pocket—clutching something.

The key, Jed guessed.

"Are you . . . all right?" Lyle asked, a stiffness to his voice.

"I'm fine," Jed said, climbing to his feet. "Just blacked out for a second, I guess."

"I see." Lyle removed his hand from his pocket. "Maybe you should lie down."

Jed stared at the pocket as if it held a shatterbox instead of a key.

"No really, I'm fine," Jed repeated.

Lyle didn't respond. Suspicion darkened his eyes as they narrowed on Jed. He opened his mouth, but before he had a chance to speak, Jed quickly cut in.

"You're right. I probably should lie down. Maybe it's all this training. I think I'm just worn out."

"Hmm . . ." Lyle muttered, his fingers drumming against his pocket and the object inside.

Jed tried not to look at the motion and instead gave Lyle an exhausted look. "I'm pretty tired."

Lyle nodded slowly but didn't respond. Jed wondered if the suspicion in Lyle's face had always been there or if Jed was just now seeing it for the first time.

Finally, Lyle spoke. "Get some rest. I have . . . an important task for you to do in the morning."

Jed

The *Endeavor*'s windows were black with night. Jed had returned to his quarters, but despite Lyle's command, he hadn't rested a bit. For hours he listened to the sound of the thrumming engine, the light clinks as dragonflies tinkered with bulkheads and circuit boards, and the muted chatter of crew members. Now, however, all but the midnight navigational engineers were sound asleep, and the only noise was the dull hum of the ion battery.

Jed lifted the handle on his cabin door and peeked out into the corridor. Empty. He crept through the train cars toward Lyle's command cabin. By now, Lyle would likely be three cars farther down, sleeping in his private bunk.

No light leaked through the edges of the cabin door. Jed

tested the handle. Locked. He closed his eyes and focused on the gears and pins that made up the locking mechanism. Warmth spread through his limbs as sparks ignited, fueling his power.

A soft click sounded from the knob as the pins set into place.

Jed tried the handle again, and this time, it turned.

Starlight trickled through the windows that lined the cabin, casting shadows around the small space.

On the east wall hung the painting of the red tree that Shay had mentioned. He'd studied the painting before, the vivid red and orange leaves of a lone tree standing against an intense blue sky. The colors had seemed so unrealistic in this world of rusted metal and blackened, polluted clouds, but now, the painting promised something he felt he had been missing the whole time he'd been aboard the *Endeavor*. Now, the painting promised reality.

With a gentle tug, the painting swung on its hinges revealing a metal safe.

Jed spun the dial to the number four, then moved it back to fourteen and then forward to nineteen. He pulled on the lever and it clicked open. The safe door swayed on its hinges, pulling forward to reveal a simple wooden box with a single pair of spectacles inside.

"Riggs," he said aloud. The word came out without his knowing why he said it or what it meant. *Riggs what?*

Carefully, glancing over his shoulder at the door, Jed pulled out the spectacles. The two golden frames surrounding the clear glass of the spectacles had tiny numbers carved into them, counting upward from one to ninety-nine. He clicked one of the frames forward, moving the number to one, and then on to two, and then to three. He moved the other as well, and then checked the note he had written himself: 14-75. He twisted the left rim dial to fourteen, and then the right side to seventy-five.

As he put the spectacles on his face, Jed's vision changed. The *Endeavor* was gone. Lyle's cabin was gone. It was different from the shared vision he had with Shay. In those visions, he'd been inside her head, feeling, smelling, tasting, and touching everything from her perspective. This time, it was as if he were a ghostly onlooker, still inside his own body, but invisible to all those around him as he stepped back in time to watch the past.

Lyle

Jed found himself in a room surrounded by gold and glass. Large domed windows on the ceiling leaked radiant sunlight and showed a bright blue sky. Lyle sat at a glass table in the center of a workshop. He wore no skin—only gold. Everything was gold: gears, cogs, sprockets, springs, wires, switches, levers, pulleys, disks, and spindles. All gold. It was a cluttered and busy workshop, but not dirty. No grime or oil marred the golden surfaces.

As Lyle glanced through the doming windows, Jed stepped sideways awkwardly, conscious of being an interloper even though he couldn't be seen. Peeking out a side window, he saw a new world below him unlike any he'd encountered in this junkyard before—one that made him feel at home.

He and Lyle stood at the top of a large stone tower. Its brown sides were covered in woven green ivy with waxen leaves sprouting every which way. Below it grew gardens—rows and rows of plants, meadows of flowers, and seas of trees waving softly in the light, sweet breeze. Cozy stone cottages dotted the landscape, surrounded by even more foliage and dappled by the sunlight shining through the leaves. It was warm, and friendly, and beautiful.

Lyle returned to his work. He picked up a needlelike instrument with one hand and lowered a set of magnifying spectacles over his eyes with the other. A small object came into focus. It was a spark with amber glowing in its core. Lyle shifted the tool closer. He studied the magnified spark, scanning it for answers. He paused on a small protrusion. His practiced, steady hands inched the tool closer. He poked the facets around the protrusion. The spark brightened and dimmed at the lightest touch, shifting color from a deep amber to a soft blue. He expertly dissected another facet and the spark turned a rich sapphire color.

A light knock rapped from the workshop's door. Lyle set the tools down on the glass table. He removed his magnifying spectacles and looked up. "I'm busy," he called. "Please come back later."

No answer came. Another knock sounded.

"Whatever it is, check with my assistant. I'm not to be bothered right now."

He reached up to pull down the magnification spectacles, but the knock came yet again.

He sighed and marched over to the door. "I said," he began, opening the door, "come back la—"

He froze. Two rows of golden knights stood with their backs to the wall. "Presenting Her Highness, Queen Calliope," one of the guards said. It was the first time Jed had ever seen her—the first time he had even realized such a person might exist—and he and Lyle reacted in the same way, their mouths dropping open.

Jed moved closer, driven forward by curiosity. The queen's golden face was astonishing. The golden sprockets and gears that formed the contours of her jaw were so small he couldn't tell where one began and another ended. It was as if it weren't made of gold at all, but instead smooth skin. She was the most beautiful thing Jed had ever seen.

"Your Majesty," Lyle said, kneeling to the floor.

She extended her hand, taking his. "Please," she said, "no need for that. My name is Calliope."

"I'm Lyle," he said, standing unsteadily.

"It's nice to meet you, Lyle," she said. Her voice had a clear metallic ring to it. "I've heard a lot about you. The other gear-smiths praise your work. They call you an innovator, inventor, and visionary."

"I don't know what to say," he said. "Thank you."

She smiled at him. The tens of thousands of gears in her cheeks flowed perfectly as they dimpled with expression. "You're probably wondering why I'm here," she said. She stepped forward into the workshop. Lyle bumbled aside, and Jed scooted away, too. Her figure moved with an ethereal grace, nearly floating across the floor.

"I've heard much about your experiments," she said. "We have need in the palace for your talents."

"The palace?" Lyle's voice sounded unsteady.

She nodded once. "I've heard that you've enhanced a life spark, thus giving it the ability to push and pull objects. Is that true?"

"Yes," Lyle said, his tone suddenly excited. "Would you like to see?"

"I would," Calliope said, a gentle smile in her voice.

He scrambled back to the glass table with the glowing spark. "I'll need a minute to calibrate the ion flux beam," he said, cranking the lever and plugging a cable into a socket. A machine lowered from the ceiling. A nozzle aimed at the spark.

Lyle flipped a switch, and a beam of violet light shot from the nozzle and struck the spark. The spark glowed as nearby scraps of junk began to wiggle. The queen and Jed both watched with interest. Lyle turned the dial slowly, studying the vibrating pieces. Bit by bit, he increased the power, and more scraps slid toward the spark. Just before the moving pieces reached the table, he cranked the dial off.

Calliope eyed the scraps. "Remarkable," she said.

Lyle then recalibrated the ion flux beam and turned the dial in the opposite direction. The beam shot out of the nozzle and struck the spark again. This time, the debris pushed away from the spark.

Lyle turned off the machine and excitedly stepped toward Calliope. "This is just the beginning," he said. "We can do so much more with sparks. Far more than pushing and pulling. I believe we can connect sparks to . . . our souls."

Calliope tilted her head. "What do you mean?"

Lyle lifted his arm. "If I want to clench my fingers into a fist, then the spark in my mind connects with the gears in my joints and my fingers curl into a ball." He closed his fingers into a fist. "What if the spark in my mind could connect with other things? Things that aren't even touching my body? The work I've been doing on life sparks will allow us to connect to everything around us. We'll control our environment without even touching it. I could turn bits and pieces of metal into extensions of my arms or legs."

Calliope's eyes sparkled. "You can do this? You are sure of it?"

"I'm almost positive," Lyle said. "I feel so close. I've worked a lifetime on this. The breakthroughs my team has made in the last year are extraordinary. We've petitioned the palace for more funding, but . . ." He shook his head.

Calliope considered Lyle. She touched her chin and squinted. "How much do you know about the relic raids?" she asked.

"Well," Lyle said, "I've heard rumors of coppers and irons, trying to infiltrate the gold city and steal our relics," Lyle said. "Glittertales to scare younglings, if you want my opinion."

"I wish they *were* rumors and glittertales," Calliope said. "But it's worse. Coppers and irons are greedy. They want everything. Our spies tell us the irons are planning an invasion."

"Invasion?" Lyle glanced at one of the windows as if to

look for warships flying toward him. "We've never shown aggression. Why would they attack us? It's—"

"Humans are never satisfied. Their greed is boundless. The more relics they steal, the more they want. We have tried to negotiate, but they know their forces are superior. And so, they threaten us, and we have no means to fight back."

"Are they planning a full attack?"

Calliope nodded. "We believe so. The only thing slowing them down is one another. Right now, coppers and irons are fighting, but it's only a matter of time before they come for us. We need your help."

"Me?" Lyle asked. "How I can help?"

Calliope motioned to a guard. The guard walked forward, a long scroll in her hands. She placed the scroll on the glass table and began to unroll it.

Lyle leaned over to study the tangle of lines, measurements, and numbers. Jed inched closer and strained to see but didn't dare get too close. This memory invasion thing was still too weird.

The scroll showed a large pile of junk. Lyle checked the proportions and gasped. Jed squeezed in even closer and felt his eyes bug, too. The shape on the page was scaled to be nearly three thousand feet tall and seven hundred feet wide at its base. Lyle leaned closer and realized that all the junk was the same: lawn mowers. It was an enormous pile of lawn mowers.

"These blueprints," he said. "I don't understand. What is this?"

"Our new guardian," Calliope said.

Lyle squinted at the blueprints again. He shook his head. "It doesn't make sense. According to this," he said, touching a spot on the page, "whatever this thing is, it's over half a mile high? That's as tall as a mountain."

Calliope nodded slowly. "Yes. It is. A mountain that you will bring to life to defend our home."

Lyle stared at her. "A mountain?" he repeated. She nodded again. "A whole mountain? That's impossible. I can't lift an entire mountain with that." He motioned to the spark on the table.

"We don't want you to lift the mountain," she said, "we want you to control it."

"Control a mountain?" Lyle asked.

Calliope smiled and nodded again. "Can you do it?" She gently placed her hand on his shoulder.

"I—I don't know. Maybe. But . . . I'd need hundreds of life sparks—maybe thousands. Perhaps if I wired them together to generate more power."

"Lawnmower Mountain is our top priority. You have full palace funding and any assistance you require." The queen's smile broadened. Her face was so gentle and kind. "We're counting on you."

"I'll do my best," Lyle said. He glanced over at the blueprints again. "Why lawn mowers?"

Calliope hesitated before answering. "Aside from their obvious offensive potential, we decided that with such power, precautionary measures must be taken," she said. "If we successfully turn an entire mountain into this city's guardian, then that kind of power would be truly terrifying. No one person should wield such dominance unchecked. The lawn mowers are our safeguard."

"Safeguard how?" Lyle asked.

"They will be wired together. Should the palace court deem it necessary at any point, we can simultaneously activate them as a self-destruct protocol. The blades will grind the guardian itself to dust if need be. But I hope it will never come to that."

Jed felt the weight of responsibility on Lyle. An equal measure of pride, excitement, and prestige stormed across the gearsmith's face as he stared into the queen's golden eyes. Jed tugged off the spectacles as the vision faded. He held them gingerly, wondering why Shay had suggested he watch that vision.

Hoping for answers, he quickly adjusted the dials to the next memory in the series that Shay had given him: 16-16. Color returned to the spectacles as he placed them on his face. Once again, he stepped into Lyle's memory as a silent, unseen observer.

Lyle

Jed and Lyle were back in the workshop, but the space was different. Time had passed. The glass windows above were sprayed with cracks, and some had broken entirely. The gold city below was ravaged. Black char coated the crumbling rooftops. In the distance stood a mountain.

Lawnmower Mountain was finished.

Lyle's workshop was in disarray. Half-finished projects lay scattered about the room. The once clear glass desk was spotted with grime and cluttered with tools. In the center of the desk lay a golden skeleton. Sparks filled its chest. Thick cables plugged into the head. The cables snaked over the edge of the table, along the floor, and out the window—all the way to the base of the mountain.

"Set the coils to forty-eight cycle charges," Lyle said to no one in particular. People scrambled around in the background, pulling levers and plugging cords into sockets.

"Fire on my command," Lyle said.

He motioned for action. A beam of light shot from the ceiling and struck the sparks in the golden skeleton. Lyle watched Lawnmower Mountain through the window. "Come on," he whispered. Jed could see the anticipation and hope building in Lyle as the mountain began to rumble. But just as some of the lawn mowers started to move, sparks burst from the golden skeleton and the mountain fell still.

A knock tapped at the door. Lyle rubbed his eyes and called behind him. "Come in."

Queen Calliope entered with her guards. "The Ninth Legion has fallen," she said. "Another four thousand soldiers are dead. The palace has lost nearly an eighth of our forces. We need the guardian. Now."

The sweetness that Jed had heard in her voice was gone. There was no gentleness or kindness. It had been replaced with panic and fear. She glanced at the table, examining the golden skeleton. "Why is it a child?"

"It's special," Lyle said, resting a hand on the skeleton's golden head. "I built it with the capacity to grow—not only physically, but in capabilities as well. It has a unique gift to adapt, to grow, as more sparks are added to its core."

"This isn't time for . . . elegance," she said. "We need results."

Lyle nodded quickly. "You're asking me to animate an

entire mountain. This vessel can do it, but it needs time to grow. And . . . I'm going to need more sparks. A lot more."

Calliope turned to her chief scribe. "Recover the sparks from the soldiers and bring them here immediately."

"Yes, my lady," the scribe said.

"You'll have your sparks," Calliope said to Lyle. "Now get my mountain working."

Lyle

Memory two now exhausted, Jed *had* to keep watching. He quickly adjusted the memory spectacles to 19-3.

. . .

There was barely anything left of Lyle's workshop, and the countryside was in ruins. On the glass table before Lyle lay the golden skeleton. Now its body was densely crusted with life sparks.

"Well?" Calliope said.

She, like Lyle, had a haggard and tired demeanor. But there was something different about Lyle in this vision. . . . His eyes seemed darker and more filled with obsession. Wires ran from his head and into the golden skeleton's.

"I'm trying something new," Lyle said. "I've fused my *own* spark to the vessel's so I can more precisely control it."

Lyle flipped a switch and concentrated on Lawnmower Mountain. Energy rushed through him, then through the cables connected to the golden body. Lyle opened his hand and lifted his right arm. The mountain rumbled, and a section of mowers began to lift, rising up in the shape of an arm.

Lyle risked a glance at Queen Calliope. Her eyes widened, and she began to smile. A loud pop echoed in the room and a surge of electricity blasted back through the cables. Lyle shrieked as the energy electrocuted his head.

"Ahhh!" he screamed, ripping the cables from his skull. A blast knocked him backward and he lay there, clutching his head. The power died, and the mountain fell still once again.

Calliope's expression melted into despair. "We're doomed," she said.

Lyle shook his head and unsteadily tried to rise. "No. Wait. There might . . ." He swayed in place, massaging the burn marks on his head. "There might be another way. I've been working on something else—a contingency plan in case I couldn't get the mountain working."

"Something else?" Calliope said, a frustrated anger creasing the delicate gold in her face. "We stand on the precipice of annihilation and you're working on 'something else'?"

"Hear me out," Lyle pleaded. "I've found a way to replace the soldiers we've lost—"

"Do you have any idea how many soldiers we've lost?" she snapped.

"Ninety-four thousand," he said.

"And we've given every spark to you! You hold our entire civilization in your workshop, and you've been working on side projects! How could you do this to me? To our people?"

Lyle stared at the ground. Fury burned in his face. His left eye twitched erratically as if it no longer worked properly. The more Calliope spoke, the less he seemed to hear. Jed had never seen this in him before. It was as if the electrical shock had damaged him in some way.

"Look at me," Calliope said sharply. "The humans are insatiable. They've plundered our wealth and technology, but it's not enough; it's *never* enough for them! Now they're slaughtering our people—shattering us into bits of golden scrap that they use for trinkets and useless machines. The gears of our brothers and sisters are being used to power turbines . . . *turbines*! We are merely a resource to these monsters. They don't see us as living creatures; they see us as tools. If we can't stop them soon, we're all dead. There are barely five thousand golds left in the world. We have no army, and soon we will have no home. We trusted you. *I* trusted you. You assured me that you could do this."

"I still can." His eye twitched awkwardly again. "I'm close. I promise. But I—"

"No!" Calliope said. "I'm shutting down your operation. Kolador Tash has been developing his own solution. He claims he can activate the mountain without sparks."

"Tash? Tash is a fool!" Lyle said, slamming his fist into the table. Calliope jumped at the uncharacteristic burst of anger. "He doesn't know the difference between a flux jumper and a neutron displacer! I've seen his plans—on more than one occasion. Sure, he can animate the mountain . . . for two weeks, four at best. I've run the numbers. In less than a month, his design will blow every capacitor in the mountain. It'll be a dead hunk of metal! He'll ruin everything! He'll waste years of effort from thousands of golds who sacrificed their lives building the guardian."

"Four weeks of operation is four weeks more than you've given us."

"I can do it," Lyle pleaded. "Just give me more time."

"You've had your time, and you've failed."

"No. You must see what else I have. I can—"

"Enough," Calliope said. "If all we have is four weeks, then maybe it's time to evacuate. You will find somewhere else—a place where no one will find us."

"We shouldn't have to run," Lyle said. "We should be the ones slaughtering them! Just hear me out and you'll see that we won't have to go anywhere."

Calliope stared at Lyle as if she no longer knew him. "Bring all the sparks to the palace by nightfall." She opened her mouth as if to say more, but she shook her head and left instead.

The room was silent. The workers stood perfectly still.

"Out!" Lyle shouted. "Everyone out!"

One by one, workers scrambled away. When the room was empty, Lyle sank to the floor. He rubbed his twitching eye, but when it didn't stop twitching, he slapped the side of his face over and over and over, until the eye finally went still.

Jed stood silently by, watching to see what Lyle would do

next. Lawnmower Mountain was astonishing, but he understood the urgency of the situation, too. And somehow Lyle had gotten his sparks working, hadn't he? Jed himself was proof of that.

"I'll show you," Lyle muttered to himself, opening his eyes and staring at the far wall with steely resolve. "Tash, Calliope, all of you. I'll save you from yourselves."

As Jed watched, Lyle clambered to his feet, locked the workshop door, and walked to a large wooden crate. He pushed the crate aside and opened the trapdoor hidden below it. Stairs led into darkness. Jed hurried to follow as Lyle made his way to the bottom of the tower. Light flooded the space as Lyle switched on a light. A hall of iron and copper corpses met his—and Jed's—eyes.

The corpses were patched together with wires, plating, and workshop scraps.

Jed recalled what Lyle had said about life sparks and dread. The golds required an entire spark to animate. Humans, on the other hand, required barcly a sliver. Once he patched up their fleshy bodies with metal scraps, he'd managed to awaken every one of these bodies with a single, shattered life spark.

As Lyle walked in the middle of them, the corpses began to shift. Dead eyes began to open.

"Admiral?" the body nearest him said. "We've been quiet like you asked, but we're bored. Do we get to kill something yet?"

Jed watched a wicked glint form in Lyle's newly darkened expression.

"Yes. It's time," Lyle said. "You get to kill a lot of things."

Lyle

Jed hesitantly set the spectacles' dial to the last memory.

He found himself beside Lyle as they flew at the front of his undead armies. The sky was black with smoke and death. Townships burned at the edges of the horizon. Directly ahead, dreadnoughts bombarded a township with shatterkeg volleys. A whistling sounded overhead. Jed ducked as a wing of falcons soared above them. Dreadnoughts fired shatterflak into the cluster of ships, obliterating them into bits of scrap.

"Focus fire on the township's center," Lyle said to one of his dread lieutenants.

The shatterkeg volleys shifted in unison and pelted the city. Jed watched as the township cracked into two halves and fell from the sky.

Lyle nodded coldly. "Send a message to the fleet," he said to the lieutenant. "We will leave two ghostnoughts to gather the dead. The rest of the fleet will move on Sunset Port immediately before word reaches them that we're near."

Jed ripped the spectacles from his face. He couldn't watch any more. The death . . . the screaming . . . the smoke.

"I need to leave. Now," he whispered just loud enough for Sprocket to hear from his backpack.

"Dowwwn to junnnk," she responded.

Jed made his way to the dark training box. He gripped the lever that Lyle had used and pulled.

The box's floor creaked apart, spilling dim light into the space. Light glittered over the junk piles below as the sun rose from behind its horizon. He'd been inside Lyle's memories for longer than he'd thought.

"Well," he said to Sprocket. "Here goes."

With a deep breath, he cinched the straps on the backpack and leaped from the *Endeavor* into open air.

Jed

Jed fell toward the piles below. Fear blasted through him. What was he thinking? What if he couldn't activate the sparks? Wind whipped past his face as he stared, terrified, at the blur of junk. Morning sunlight glinted off the metal, making their edges look even sharper.

He tried to activate his sparks, but his fear made it impossible to concentrate. He could imagine Lyle's voice snickering at him, telling him that if he'd only used his special key . . .

SPLAGHETTI rang in his mind, and right then, he remembered what the *S* stood for: self-reliance.

"No," Jed said aloud to the deadly piles. "I don't need some rusty key. I'm strong enough without it." Heat exploded through him as his sparks blazed to life. Pulling energy from the mutiny sparks, he pressed against the ground below until he slowed and landed softly.

Heroism. "*H* is for heroism, Sprocket," he said over his shoulder. "I think jumping out of a flying train toward certain death counts, don't you?"

"Funnn," Sprocket buzzed.

Jed looked up in sky as the *Endeavor* flew on without them.

As the morning sun continued to rise, he scanned the sky until he spotted a small township floating in the west. Small was good. Small would help him hide from Lyle until Shay could pick him up.

Staring at the distant city, he smiled to himself. He was ready for a little *I*: insanity.

He mutinied himself into the air, pushing diagonally against the junk below. Wind rushed past his face. His hair fluttered in the breeze. Stomach clenching with the momentum, he almost immediately regretted his brash rocketing upward. But the feeling was so empowering. It was as if the whole world were his to explore.

"We're flying!" he yelled to Sprocket. The words felt impossible. Unbelievable. Exhilarating. Liberating.

The clouds hanging overhead were puffy, white, and inviting. Excitement buzzed through Jed as an idea taunted him. He dove back toward the ground. Then he flared his sparks. Metal squealed and compressed below him, smashing together to form a small crater. He pulled more energy from his mutiny sparks. His body changed directions and shot into the air. He mutinied against the junk, rocketing higher and higher.

The momentum carried him into the clouds.

"Oooh!" Sprocket's tinny voice squeaked from Jed's backpack.

He wished he could float there forever. In the peaceful clouds, away from everything.

But then he sank back through the clouds and plummeted toward the earth.

His heart thumped nervously as he wondered whether he had enough power to slow his fall. As soon as he could sense the junk he began mutinying his body away from it. Gears and capacitors heated with the effort, and he barely slowed.

Panic welled inside him as he tried to pull more energy from the mutiny sparks. He slowed a little, but he'd accidentally depleted his sparks from the jump to the clouds. He cringed as the junk below sped toward him.

"Come on," he said through gritted teeth, forcing as much power from the mutiny sparks as he could.

Energy drained from him, and instead of feeling heat, there was an overwhelming chill of emptiness.

It wasn't enough.

An all-encompassing pain ripped across his flesh as he slammed clear through a toppled wardrobe. His golden body punched into the junk like a bullet hitting water. Skin ripped from his arms, legs, and face. Pain seared through him, and when he finally stopped tearing through the scrap, his body felt like a crumpled soda can.

Jed groaned and tried to move his arms. They were tangled in a vacuum cleaner cord and pinned underneath a bookshelf.

His legs wouldn't move either, but he couldn't even see what was holding them in place.

Everything hurt.

He lay there motionless. His head throbbed, his bones ached, his freshly torn skin burned.

"Sprocket?" he mumbled, trying to look over his shoulder at the red backpack. He'd hit the junk face-first, so maybe she was okay on his back.

A weak chittering noise answered. "Gzzz."

Despite the agony he smiled.

"You okay back there?" he asked.

The can buzzed, and a metallic ring responded with something Jed could have sworn sounded like, "Yezzz."

"So how do we get out?" Jed asked.

Sprocket didn't respond.

He sighed. "Yeah. This is a tough one."

He tried moving again, but junk engulfed him. The most he could do was to fall asleep and hopefully recharge his sparks. Before he could think any more about it, he was already waking up from sleep. He didn't know how long he'd slept, but the sun was now high in the sky. Bits of energy swam through his sparks. He tried shifting in place, but too much junk still held him in his crumpled position.

He reached for the refreshed energy supply. Activating the mutiny spark, he pushed away the junk that pinned him in place. Scraps shifted from his body, creating a small pocket of space. He sighed as the pressure abated and he could once again move.

"Let's get out of here," he said to Sprocket.

"Zzzok!" she agreed.

Jed wiggled and squirmed his way through the tightly packed junk above. He conserved as much of his power as possible—only using it when he couldn't squeeze between scraps.

When he finally reached the top of the junk, he rolled onto a kitchen table and sighed. The bright sun overhead highlighted the cuts, scrapes, and bruises that covered him in a big ball of pain. Gold metal glistened through torn skin.

"Bzzzooorrrk," Sprocket buzzed from his backpack.

He carefully unzipped the pack and took her out. Her tin can body was ruthlessly dented, and more than half of her legs were crooked.

"I'm sorry," he said to her. "I didn't mean for that to happen to you . . . or to me. I was being reckless."

"Gazzzabok," she hummed in an *It's okay, I know you didn't mean to* tone.

"I wonder if . . ." Jed trailed off as he turned her over in his hands. "Hmm."

He closed his eyes and felt the pieces around him. They spoke to him . . . called to him. "Wings," he said.

Energy flowed from his batteries into the rally spark. Junk tumbled toward him. He opened his eyes to find a Ping-Pong paddle and a Frisbee in his lap. "These could work," he said.

He closed his eyes again and scanned the junk. "Gears, wire, bolts, wrench, and screwdriver," he said.

A dozen objects crawled from the piles and bumbled their way toward him.

Alone, sitting there in the junk, he tinkered with Sprocket until the Ping-Pong paddle and Frisbee were securely fastened to her back. He routed his power into the life spark and poured it into the tin can. The wings began to flutter.

"Bzzziiinnn!" Sprocket hummed excitedly as she lifted into the air.

"Now we can both fly," Jed said. With that, he activated the mutiny spark and lifted himself into the air. As he glided over the piles, Sprocket flew beside him.

Jed

J ed was convinced of several things: Flying was the greatest
thing ever; Lyle was crazy; Lyle must be looking for him
by now; and, he had to save the world. He also needed somewhere to lay low. A little help wouldn't hurt either.

As Jed flew across the junkyard, a dot appeared at the edge
of the horizon.

Township, Jed thought.

"Zzzzgaaandip," Sprocket buzzed nervously.

"I think you're right," Jed agreed. "I can't imagine they're
going to be too friendly to a talking can and a skin-wearing
robot."

He landed about a mile away in a mound of metal. "I'm
going to need to cover up these cuts," he said to Sprocket. "At

least until the skin heals." He considered his options, glancing around. Then a thought struck him.

"Glue," he said, reaching out his hand.

A golf club zipped forward from the junk and smacked him in the face.

"Not gluuueee," Sprocket said.

Jed rubbed his forehead. "Thanks. I kind of realized that."

He tried again. One spatula, three books, and two bottles of shampoo later, a yellow plastic bottle of wood glue flew into his palm. Jed stared at it, delighted. He unplugged the bottle and began filling each of his wounds and cuts with wood glue until every bit of gold was covered.

Once masked, he raised himself back up and carefully approached the distant floating city. Bits of his memory returned as he stared at the city. He remembered going to other cities with . . . a tug crew. Faces flickered in his mind. Bog . . . Kizer . . . Riggs . . . Pobble . . . Shay . . . *Sprocket.*

A cold emptiness chilled his heart. "Sprocket," he whispered.

"Yezzz," the can buzzed.

He looked at her. "You died," he said. "He killed you. Lyle. How could I forget that?"

The memory stung. He missed Sprocket. Jed slunk to the ground as new images flooded his mind. His parents. A memory. Years ago, when the three of them went to the opera. "Roast beef sandwiches," he whispered. The memory felt distant, as if Jed was looking through a foggy window dotted with rain. "We brought them inside of a coat."

And then, as if the window shattered, the scene opened with rich color and vivid detail.

"Ryan, you didn't . . ." his mother said. She had porcelain skin and pink cheeks. Her hair was short and disobedient. Jed wanted so badly to see the details of her face, but it was still just a white-and-rosy blur. His father gave her a sheepish smirk. "Open your coat," she demanded. He shook his head like a child hiding a cookie. "Open it now," she said, giving him her best folded-arms glare.

His father looked to the left and then to the right. He opened his coat to reveal three bottles of root beer and three paper bags hanging by clothespins.

"This is the opera," she said. The words seemed like they were trying to sound scolding despite the faint laugh creeping into her lips.

"Exactly. And in all the times that we've been to the opera, how many of those times did we have access to root beer and roast beef sandwiches?"

"I count zero," Jed said.

"And you would be correct," his father said. "Zero indeed. It's time for things to change, Mary. And when things must change, what do we do?"

"We change them," Jed said.

"That we do, Jed," his father said. "That we do."

His father rested his hand on Jed's shoulder. His face sharpened.

He gave Jed a single nod and smiled before closing his trench coat and holding out his arm for Jed's mother to take. Still trying to stifle the grin that dimpled her cheeks, she hooked her arm in his, and the three of them headed to their booth.

Jed's mind felt alive. More memories prickled the recesses

of his brain. *Flour fights in the kitchen . . . pineapple upside-down cake . . . Lemon Saturday . . .*

"I remember them," he said to Sprocket the can. "Both of them. Ryan wasn't my kidnapper, he was my father. I remember my home. It was redbrick, and I helped my dad build the fence in the backyard. I remember how the wood smelled as we sawed the ends of the planks."

Like a cascading waterfall, his hidden memories began filling his soul with a lifetime—his lifetime.

Jed

Jed stepped into the shadow of the township overhead. With a deep breath, he shot up into the sky toward the floating city. To his left, one of the docking ports was empty. He pulled himself to the edge of the port. Despite his best efforts, he smacked the side of the dock but managed just enough purchase to swing himself over the edge.

A sign at the end of the dock read: WELCOME TO RIGGER HOLLOW.

Jed focused on Shay's image in his mind. "Rigger Hollow," he whispered. He had no idea how to link to her, but he had to try. "Rigger Hollow," he said again, closing his eyes. He repeated the name over and over.

The township was small. It was a speck in the sky compared to Lunkway—a mere blink and passersby would miss it entirely. Hopefully, Lyle would blink.

Jed walked the main street, self-consciously hoping that none of his gold was showing. He spotted a restaurant called Chog's. Across the street was another restaurant called Velpin's.

A burly man stood outside of Chog's with a crate of canned chicken.

"Hey," Jed said. "Are you Chog?"

The man nodded. "Can I help you?"

His memories back, Jed longed for the opportunity to cook again. "I was wondering if you had any job openings," he said.

"Scram," Chog said. "The Rigger orphanage is down the road. You can pick up a can of expired beets from them just like every other urchin beggar."

Jed liked a lot of foods that other kids didn't. Mushrooms, asparagus, salmon, even the occasional anchovy. But beets were where he drew the line. The wicked little red monsters tasted like dirt. Bitter, horrid dirt. He didn't know how long he'd have to wait for Shay and his dad, but he wasn't going to do so eating beets.

Beets did not equal survival.

"Yeah. That's not really going to work for me."

Chog shrugged. "Whatever, kid. Not my problem."

"No. It's not. But it could be your opportunity."

At the word *opportunity*, Chog set down his crate of canned chicken. "What do you mean, 'opportunity'?"

Jed looked across the street at Velpin's, which was full of people talking, laughing, and eating. Chog's restaurant looked sad and desolate by comparison. "I think Velpin is doing all right for himself."

Chog glared at the colorful restaurant. "That slug has been here less than three weeks! You want to know how long I've been here? Twenty-four years! Twenty-four years I've run a fine establishment. I know half the town. I call my customers by name. But then Velpin throws up some shiny lights and a bit of paint, and now my place is emptier than a gutted slug."

"I'll bet you a can of chicken and a few swigs of pineapple juice that I can get every customer in sight back at your tables," Jed said.

. . .

Jed stirred the coconut carrot soup with a spatula.

"What in slug clunk are you doing?" Chog asked. He leaned over the pot and inhaled.

"Would you like a taste?" Jed asked. He dipped a spoon into the creamy soup and lifted it toward Chog's mouth. The restaurateur looked skeptically at the spoon as if it were poison. Finally, though, he took it and gave a gingerly sip. His left eyebrow raised slowly as he swished the soup around in his mouth.

"How'd you—"

"Pretty good, right?"

"I've never tasted anything like it. And I've tasted *everything*."

Jed nodded. "That probably means no one else in this city has tasted anything like it either."

Chog grinned. "We're going to make sacks of batteries with that scrap!"

"Does that mean I'm hired?" Jed asked.

Shay

"Shay," Jed's voice whispered in her mind for the thousandth time that week.

"Yes, Broken Mouse. I'm here. But, let me guess, you can't hear me. Right?"

"Shay . . . can you hear me?"

"Yep. Loud and clear. What about you? Can your teensy little mouse cars hear me?"

"Shay. Are you there?"

"That's what I thought."

"If you're there . . ."

"Yup, I'm here."

". . . I'm at a town called Rigger Hollow."

"I know. You've squeaked it at me two hundred times

189

already. And you keep squeaking and squeaking and squeaking and squeaking. We're trying to find you, but everyone in the mouseyard loves killing scritches, and we have lots and lots of scritches on our very, very scritcherly-looking boats. So . . ."

A gruff voice called from behind. "Shay? Who are you talking to?"

Shay turned around. "Oh, hi," she said to Captain Bog. "Just Jed."

"Jed?"

"Yep. He's been talking to me in my brain. Didn't I tell you?"

He slowly shook his head. "I think you forgot to mention that one."

"Oh. Well, he's been talking to me in my brain. Sometimes he sees through my eyes, too."

Bog gave her an odd look. "I thought you said that Jed just sent you a message that he was in Rigger Hollow. . . ."

"Oh, he did. A message in my head."

"In your head . . ."

"Exactly."

"Are you feeling all right, Shay?"

"I definitely *won't* be if he keeps nagging and nagging and nagging about Rigger Hollow. Every day, it's *Rigger Hollow, Rigger Hollow, Shay can you hear me, Shay I'm here*, and I don't think my brain can take it anymore."

"You're really communicating with him?"

"Not so much anymore. I think we're too far away, and his brain voice is many squeaks louder than mine. So he keeps

shouting, shouting, shouting, and I can't say anything back."
Shay released a big sigh. "It just makes me tired."

Intrigue sparked through Bog's eyes. "Has he told you
anything important? What do you know? Has he mentioned
where Lyle is? Have the coppers and irons formed an offensive
against the dread like I've been hearing from rumors? What
is their combined military strength? Do they have freighters?
How are they coordinating their supply chains?"

"Let's see . . ." Shay tapped her chin, "I *do* know lots of
things." Bog leaned in closer. "I know that . . . Jed works at a
restaurant now! It's called Chog's. Probably because Chog is
the one who made it. But, that's just *my* guess."

"A restaurant . . ." Bog said, lifting an eyebrow.

"Also, he can *fly!*" she added. "Like a mouse with wings!"

Bog sighed. "Wonderful. . . . That helps us . . . so much."

Shay beamed at him. "Oh, good. I love being a helpful
mouse."

Jed

The sweet scent of cooking oil and chicken filled Chog's kitchen. Jed had talked the restaurant owner into installing a bathtub in the restaurant. He knew there was probably a better way to make a stove, but the bathtub reminded him of the tugboat. Chog reacted the way the old crew had around fire and suggested that no one know what Jed was doing.

Within two days, word had spread about Jed's new menu. Velpin's looked nearly abandoned, and Chog had more business than he'd had in twenty-four years.

Every table was filled with an unending supply of customers.

"Two more orders of carrot coconut soup!" Chog called from the dining room.

Jed sliced open another half dozen cans of carrot puree and one can of coconut milk, then dumped them in a pot. "Give me ten minutes," he called back, adding butter, thyme, curry powder, onion, and garlic.

"Oh, and one winter minestrone, and another pea risotto."

Jed scanned the shelves for canned cannellini beans, carrots, chicken broth, kale, and pasta.

By the end of the night, he'd managed to expand the menu to include creamed spinach, potatoes with paprika and caramelized onions, cherry clafoutis, and ambrosia fruit salad. The endless stream of patrons would have left any cook exhausted. But not Jed. That night, as he lay down in his bed, all he could think of was how much he wanted to make a specialized soups menu that included Indian lentil soup, shrimp bisque, and Moroccan stew.

I'm going to need an assistant, he decided as an idea popped into his head right before closing his eyes and falling asleep.

. . .

The next day, Jed visited the beet distribution line near the orphanage to find someone to help him in Chog's kitchen. He arrived at lunchtime and found a scrawny girl sitting beside the building, gnawing on an uncooked beet.

Jed sat beside her. "Hi," he said. "I'm new in town. My name's Jed."

She looked up from her beet and gave him a curious look. "Penelope," she said. "Penny for short." She glanced at the distribution center, but the window was closed. "Oh, did you get here too late for lunchtime beets? You can have half of mine, if you'd like." She lifted the nibbled-on beet and offered it to Jed.

"Actually," Jed said, "I was wondering if *you'd* like to eat something other than beets."

Her face slumped. "They only offer beets here."

"I work at Chog's down the street," Jed said. "I'm looking for someone to help me at the restaurant while I'm cooking. Are you interested?"

"Cooking? What's cooking?"

Jed smiled. "Come on. I'll show you. And you can have all the cans of food you want."

The whole way back to Chog's, Penny stared at him suspiciously as if this was all just one big prank.

Jed led her past the line waiting outside and into the restaurant.

"Hey!" Chog shouted over his notepad as he jotted down a customer's order. "You there! I've seen you begging around here before. Get out of my place and go back to the beet distribution center."

"Actually," Jed said, "she's our new employee."

Chog glared at Jed, but he didn't argue. How could he? Jed's cooking was bringing in more business than Chog had ever had.

"Come on," Jed said to Penny. "The kitchen's back here."

He gave Penny a tour of the pantry and the restaurant, but first he gave her three whole cans of peaches. She devoured each one and slurped up its syrup almost before Jed could open the next.

"Three more sides of potato salad!" Chog called from the dining room.

"I have a special job for you," Jed said. "I need a guard."

"A guard?" Penny asked, her mouth still full of peaches.

"I need you to keep watch and make sure no one comes into the kitchen—not even Chog."

"That's it?"

"Pretty much. Only come in when I call you for a dish but never at any other time. Okay?"

She nodded. "And I can eat more peaches if I do?"

"All the peaches you want."

A grin spread across her face, and she rushed from the kitchen to stand guard immediately.

Alone in the kitchen once again, Jed smiled to himself. "This is going to be fun."

With a deep breath, he closed his eyes and lifted his arms. The kitchen with all of its cans, utensils, and dishes appeared in his mind. Their tiny threads of connection linked him to everything in the room.

"Smoked oysters," he whispered, opening his hand. His rally spark ignited, and a can shot from the pantry and slapped his empty palm.

. . .

For the first day in a week, Jed managed to keep up with the endless orders. According to Penny, Chog had frustratedly tried to bully his way into the kitchen on several occasions, but apparently Penny had stood her ground, arms folded, and refused to let him in. Jed cooked a whole pot of tortilla soup just for her and gave it to her at the end of the day—pot and all.

Before bed, he focused on Shay's image and repeated his location, over and over. He had no idea whether the messages were reaching her, but something inside him said to keep trying. He hadn't been able to reestablish a connection with her since he'd arrived.

Early the next morning, he floated down to the piles of junk. He'd been craving a Milanese risotto, but there was no saffron to be found. He knew there probably wasn't any saffron in the whole junkyard, but if there was even a chance, he had to try.

He'd been practicing every day with his ability. Alone, under the dimming sky or early in the morning, Jed closed his eyes and let his sparks awaken. Soon, invisible threads connected him to the world.

"Saffron," he whispered. The objects dissipated until there was nothing left. He nodded to himself, knowing it had been a slim chance. As he opened his eyes, a faint, almost indistinguishable object answered from far away—perhaps thousands of miles off. Curious, he lifted himself into the air and began soaring toward the signal. Sprocket buzzed alongside him as he flew. No matter how far he traveled it didn't seem to get any closer.

"Maybe I can call it to me?" he said to Sprocket.

"Mmmaybeee," she said, a hint of uncertainty in her tone.

Jed floated to the ground. He focused and powered up the

rally spark. He lightly pulled against it, but it resisted as if stuck on something. He tugged harder. It didn't move.

The image in his mind was so odd. It was like nothing he'd searched for in the past. It was like it was in the junkyard, but then it . . . wasn't.

"No," he whispered. It wasn't in the junkyard at all. It was beyond the fringe. That's why he couldn't see it.

Excitement welled inside him. Could he pull something from beyond the fringe? "Here," he said. The saffron shuddered, and Jed's excitement grew. He blasted the rally spark, yanking the saffron toward him.

He opened his eyes.

Dark clouds swirled overhead. Jed's stomach clenched. His heart raced and sweat beaded all over his body. Warning sirens rang from Rigger Hollow's watchtowers. Even from this far away, Jed could hear distant cries from the townspeople. Guilt swirled through him. All he'd wanted was a bottle of saffron. He didn't realize that pulling it from beyond the fringe would cause a junkstorm.

Jed

Rigger Hollow's propellers tilted away from the storm, and the township began to move. People yelled as the storm-side barriers lifted at the edge of the township. Something zipped toward Jed. He reflexively held up his hand to shield himself. A small bottle of saffron landed in his palm.

"Let's get back there," he said to Sprocket.

"Huuurrry."

Jed lifted himself into the air to follow the retreating city just as junk from the storm began crashing below. The sound was deafening. Winds tossed his body from side to side as he tried to keep himself steady. A chessboard flung past him and exploded against the ground.

Jed peeked over his shoulder. The storm was growing

larger. He sped faster through the air, quickly closing the gap to the township.

This time as he ascended to the broken docking station, he didn't have to worry about being seen. Everyone was either running for cover or operating stations to bolster the township defenses.

"Reroute capacitors two-oh-nine through eight-oh-seven," someone yelled. "I want as much power to the underside turbines as I can get!"

Jed couldn't see who was speaking through the dust and wind-blown debris.

"Hiiide," Sprocket said, concern wobbling in her tone.

Jed shook his head. "I'm not going to find cover until the township is safe."

Engineers rushed back and forth from a building with a lightning bolt warning symbol on its doors. They dragged cables from the building to the main deck, where ladders extended to the turbines. Jed bolted toward the doors and slipped inside the building.

Power cells lined the walls. Jed found a retractable cable at the end of a shelving unit. He pulled the cable free, took off his shirt, and plugged it into his chest. "You need more power?" he whispered to the cables. "Here you go." His sparks released some of their energy into the cables. Light swelled in the shelving units until the cells were pulsing with energy.

"Hunnngry batterrriezzz," she said, fluttering over to one of the glowing walls.

Each of the shelves on the wall were connected by linking

capacitors. Jed found the main cable and plugged it into his chest. The building hummed as Jed lent his power to the city.

"The battery house is . . . *gaining* power," a confused voice called from outside. "What's going on in there?"

"I don't know," another voice called, "but reroute everything you got to the east thrusters. Let's get out of here!"

The storm had doubled in size by the time Jed was back outside. The township was accelerating away from the storm, but not fast enough.

"There has to be something I can do," he mumbled to Sprocket.

"Something sooon," she added. "Biiig storrrm."

Jed climbed up the township's railing and hung over the edge of the city. He poured what energy he had left into the mutiny sparks. He could feel a deep hum as the spark awaited direction. He focused on the piles of junk near the base of the junkstorm, then pushed.

His body compressed against the edge of the township as the force of his spark propelled him backward into it. Distant pieces of junk squished into one another as he pushed against them. Steadily, he dumped more of his power into the spark. His body pressed harder and harder against the township. The mutiny spark turned his body into an engine more powerful than all the propellers underneath him.

"We are moving faster," someone shouted. "I don't understand."

"That's not possible. I'm showing new power failures in

cells one-oh-nine through two-twelve. We should be slowing down."

Jed poured everything he had into his sparks. The township accelerated, flying through the sky as if it were a ship. His expended capacitors heated with a painful searing sensation. But as the power left him, so did the heat, until his body was cold and empty.

Head dizzy and muscles weak, Jed climbed back onto the city before cutting off power to the mutiny spark. As he lay on his back, the township's momentum carried them away from the junkstorm and under safe skies.

Jed

By nightfall, scavenger parties had received word of the storm and arrived to loot its treasures. Iron falcons and copper wasps littered the sky. Men and women crawled all over the fresh junk, scouring its contents for trinkets.

The influx of people below them made Jed nervous. "Come on, Shay," he whispered to himself. "Where are you?"

If he didn't get out of here soon, Lyle would find him again.

Chog's restaurant was mostly undamaged, and Rigger Hollow was filled with so many scavengers that the streets could barely hold them all. All day long, every chair and table at Chog's was filled with hungry scavengers. Jed worked frantically to fill customer orders, and Penny worked diligently at her post.

"Two orders of minestrone," Chog called to Jed. "And I got someone here asking if the cook can make 'tomatoey chicken stuff covered in slug killer.' His words, not mine."

"What?" Jed asked.

Chog just shrugged.

A memory surfaced in Jed's mind. The first time he'd made food for the tugboat crew, Pobble was horrified when he used salt. He called it "slug killer." Jed sat down the can of peaches he'd been holding and peered out of the kitchen at the crowd. There, standing in line and staring hungrily at his exotic menu was—

"Pobble!" Jed shouted. Pobble's Ping-Pong-ball eyes opened as widely as they would go, and his mouth dropped open.

"Golden Boy?" Riggs said from behind him.

"No clunking way," Kizer said, poking his head out from behind his crewmates with a stunned look of disbelief in his eyes.

"How did you guys find me?" Jed asked.

"Find you?" Pobble asked. "We came here for the scavenge, just like everyone else. Heard there were a good restaurant in town. Didn't expect you to be running it."

Jed shook his head. "I'm just working here until Captain Bog comes and picks me up."

"The Captain's alive?" Kizer said, stepping forward. "What happened?"

Jed looked around. In a lower voice, he whispered, "Not here. Come on back."

He guided them to the kitchen and closed the door.

"Captain Bog's alive," Jed said. "He's going to pick me up here as soon as he can."

"What about Sprocket?" Pobble asked. "Is she here, too?" He looked around as if he might've just missed her standing there in the kitchen.

Jed's stomach sank. He shook his head.

"Where is she?" Pobble asked.

"She died," Jed said. "The dread king killed her."

"The dread king?" Riggs asked. "You saw him?"

"He's sort of my father. Kind of. Not the father I was looking for. He's the one who . . ." Jed hesitated, glancing uncomfortably at Kizer. All those times Kizer had accused him of being a dread—what was he going to do when he learned what Jed really was?

"Who *what*?" Kizer asked, suspicion raising his tone.

Jed took a deep breath. "He's the one who built me."

All three stared at Jed.

"*Built* you?" Kizer said, exactly as Jed expected.

"It's not what you think," Jed said.

The pantry door opened then, and Chog stepped out, his arms folded across his chest and his expression filled with hate.

"Hey, Chog . . ." Jed said.

"You . . . you're one of them. You's a dread," Chog said.

Jed held up his hands. "No. I'm not a dread."

"I just heard you. You told them. You ain't a human. You's a machine."

"But I'm not a dread. There's a difference."

Chog slowly shook his head. "Ain't no difference. You's a liar!"

"Chog, no," Jed pleaded. "I helped you. I saved your restaurant."

"You was gonna eat my customers. Then you was gonna eat me!"

"I wasn't going to eat anyone, I swear. I'm not what you think I am."

"Dread!" Chog shouted, running from the kitchen into the dining room. "Dread!"

The bustling dining room fell silent, and the only voice that could be heard was Chog as he continued to yell the word *dread*.

"There's a window out back," Jed said. "Come on."

Pobble, Kizer, and Riggs exchanged looks.

Jed shrugged. "You can come with me if you want," he said, "but you don't have to. Either follow me or explain to them what you were doing cavorting with a nasty dread."

Kizer opened his mouth.

Jed smirked. "Come on. Let's go," he said again.

They were out the window and halfway down the street before Chog or anyone from the dining room entered the kitchen.

"Where's the tug?" Jed asked.

Kizer gave him a hard look. "If you board our tug, we'll have the whole city watch on us. I don't want to be outrunning patrol boats for the next week."

Jed laughed. "Leave the patrol boats to me," he said.

"What's that supposed to mean?" Pobble asked.

"It means I'm not exactly the same clunkhead kid who

couldn't climb a ladder that you once knew," Jed said, smiling at Kizer.

Riggs seemed intrigued. "To *Bessie*, then," he said before Kizer could argue. Riggs motioned for them to follow. They snuck through the streets until they reached the docking port that held *Bessie*.

"You should probably hide out in the stowaway cabin until we're clear of the city—just in case word makes it to the docking guards and they start searching boats," Riggs said.

Jed nodded. "Good idea."

As they climbed aboard *Bessie*, Jed headed down the stairs to the kitchen, where he lifted the secret floor panel and descended into the stowaway cabin.

Shay's charcoal drawings covered the walls of the small compartment. Jed stared at the picture of the lemon, and a flood of nostalgia rippled through him. This was where he'd first met her. He could still remember her clutching the can of beans as if it were yesterday. They'd come so far. . . .

"Sky prop up!" Kizer called from above.

Gears churned as the ship's sky propeller lifted in place and began to spin.

Bessie lifted from the dock and hovered in the air.

"Full thrusters ahead!" Kizer yelled to Riggs. "And, Golden Boy, you're in the clear."

Jed scampered from the stowaway compartment and joined the rest of the crew on deck.

"Glad to be back?" Pobble asked.

Jed nodded. "Glad to be back."

Jed

Bessie sailed through the air away from Rigger Hollow. Jed stood at her edge and gazed into the sky as warm wind flowed over him. The tugboat wasn't his home, but the rich sense of familiarity wrapped him in a comforting hug. It felt good to be back on board. He imagined the old crew bustling about the main deck —Pobble tinkering with his fiddle while Kizer paced the bridge, hands clasped behind his back. Then he pictured Sprocket cleaning her shatterlance and shouting at Captain Bog.

He glanced to his left, where Sprocket the tin can rested on his shoulder. "I'm sorry I couldn't save you."

"Um, Jed?" Pobble said from behind.

Jed turned around, but the bard didn't need to explain why he was interrupting Jed's daydreaming. Up ahead of them, directly in their path, a stark line of dreadnoughts stretched across the horizon.

Kizer poked his head from the wheelhouse and called down to Jed. "You said Captain Bog took control of part of the dread fleet. . . . Is that *him?*"

Jed studied the blockade of vessels until he spotted a snakelike ship squirming through the ranks. The *Endeavor.* Apparently, Lyle had recalled his twenty-thousand dread from war after Jed left. . . . Jed shook his head and called back. "Those aren't Bog's. They're the old dread king's."

Kizer grabbed a lever and pulled. The tugboat slowed its movement toward the warships, hovering in the sky—a miniscule dust speck standing before an army of monsters.

"Hello, son," a voice whispered in his mind.

Lyle.

"Get out of my head," Jed whispered back.

"Huh?" Pobble asked.

"Nothing," Jed said.

Lyle's whisper returned. "I knew you'd come back to me. Now, if you don't make a scene, I'll let your friends live."

"I'm not going back to you," Jed said. "I'll never go back."

Pobble stared at him, head cocked as he watched Jed talk to the air.

"I must insist," Lyle whispered.

A boom echoed from one of the dreadnoughts. A single shot arced through the sky toward them.

Kizer wrenched a set of levers and *Bessie* turned in the air. He jammed another lever forward, and the ship shot away from the dread fleet and safely out of range from the shatterfire.

"If he's trying to ambush us," Kizer called through the bridge window, "he's doing a clunk-poor job."

Jed slowly shook his head. "He's not trying to shoot us down," he said, more to himself than to Pobble or Kizer.

Rigger Hollow's warning signs rang as the town lookouts spotted the dread army.

The dreadnoughts advanced at a steady, slow pace toward the city. Their black smoke stained the sky and engulfed them in a frothy cloud. Kizer moved *Bessie* cautiously out of range of their approach, keeping a safe distance.

"Jed?" Kizer called. "What in the clunk-covered skies is he doing?"

Jed shook his head. "I don't know."

The line of dreadnoughts pushed them all the way back to the Rigger Hollow city line. Another shot launched from one of the dreadnoughts. As it sailed through the sky, Kizer easily moved the ship out of range. But the shot had not been aimed at them. One of the buildings on the east edge of the city exploded into orange fire.

Jed's heart lurched.

Bessie backed farther away from the city, but the dreadnoughts were no longer advancing toward the tug. Shatterkegs crackled from the front of their hulls. A volley of shatterfire domed across the sky. Orange explosions blossomed throughout the floating city.

"No!" Jed yelled at Lyle. An image of the sweet orphan girl, Penny, burned into his mind. She must be so scared right now watching the rockets sail toward her home.

"These are the consequences of your choices," Lyle whispered back in his mind. Then Jed felt the voice retreat and vanish completely.

A second volley arced from the dreadnoughts, slamming into the city. As the third volley hit, several turbines began to whine and slow.

Penny . . . Jed thought to himself.

The city wilted as chunks fell away, dripping to the junk piles below. The sirens stopped wailing as the towers that still held crumbled to rubble.

"Stop it!" he yelled, but there was no answer.

The fourth volley fired at the center of the city. Shatterfire smashed down and the city cracked in two. The half closest to the tugboat tilted and fell away from the other. The turbines could no longer keep the two halves afloat.

The dreadnoughts ceased fire and stood guard as the rest of the city toppled.

"Jed," a new voice said in his mind.

Shay.

"I'm here," he said unsteadily.

"We're almost to Rigger Hollow, but it looks kind of broken. Is it broken? Are you broken?"

"You got my message," he said.

"You mean, your message*s.* All six hundred of them."

"I found the tug crew. We're safe for now," Jed said, his voice still shaking from the senseless murder in front of him. "Meet us half a sunfall from the east side of Rigger Hollow. I'll explain everything."

Jed

Coordinates set, *Bessie* began sailing toward their destination. Jed leaned against the ship's railing, still in shock from what he'd just seen. *Penny* . . . Her sweet face haunted him now when he closed his eyes. She was dead. They were all dead. He wondered if the pieces of Rigger Hollow were still on fire.

A meaty hand slapped against his shoulder. "You doin' all right, there, Jed?" Pobble said, joining them at the railing.

Jed shrugged. "I don't know. They're all . . . dead."

"It ain't your fault," Pobble said. "Ya know that, right?"

"I guess so. But it sort of feels like it is."

"Yeah. I get that." He gave Jed a curious look. "So . . . changing the subject . . . you really got scrap for bones, then?"

Jed smiled at him. "Yeah. I guess I do. I'm just one big piece of clunk."

Pobble slapped his own belly with both hands. "Nah, you ain't that big. You's got a long way to go before you can ever call you big."

Angry footsteps clomped toward them from behind. Jed turned around to find himself nose-to-nose with Kizer.

"Start talking," he said.

Jed rubbed his chin and thought for a moment. "Hm. What should we talk about? Ah, I got it: You know what goes really well with tarragon? Salmon and artichokes."

Kizer slowly shook his head.

"No, I'm serious," Jed said. "The tarragon really brings out the fish's flavor."

Kizer folded his arms and kept glaring. "I'm not in the mood, Golden Boy."

"I get it," Jed said. "Sometimes I'm not in the mood for fish, either. Tarragon also goes pretty well with veal."

Pobble snorted.

"Either start talking, or I'm going to start pulling off those scrap limbs of yours," Kizer said.

Jed assessed his arms. "That's the thing about having arms made out of scrap," he said. "They are held together quite well." He rotated his arm in a circle.

"Fine," Kizer said. "Then either you start talking, or I'll throw you off this tug."

"You've really got to work on your threats," Jed said. "I

know that used to be your thing—throwing me off the boat and all—but the thing is . . . I can sort of fly now."

Pobble's mouth dropped open, and his face lit up with a giddy excitement. "Really?" he asked with a childlike enthusiasm.

"Stop gawking at him," Kizer said. "He can't fly. He's just a smart mouth. You know that."

Jed smirked. "I'll make you a deal, Ki." He folded his arms and matched Kizer's intimidating posture. "If I can fly circles around this tug, then you have to cook lunch for Pobble, Riggs, and me. And"—he held up a finger—"you have to cook it in a bathtub. Just like old times. Fire and all."

Kizer looked from Pobble to Jed. "Liar," he said finally.

Jed stuck out his hand, ready to shake. "Do we have a deal?"

. . .

Kizer spent almost the entire trip trying to make the crew lunch in the bathtub. He hadn't said a single word to Jed since watching him soar around *Bessie* like an iron falcon. The poor man had no idea what he was doing as he mixed together canned pineapple, black beans, and creamed corn.

"I found some glasses on Lyle's ship," Jed said to Riggs. The three of them sat in wooden chairs next to the bathtub as Kizer worked. "Kind of like the ones you have," he said.

Riggs leaned forward. "You did?"

Jed nodded. "I wasn't lying when I told you all that time

ago that I didn't know where other relics were. I just didn't realize that I was one of them."

Riggs laughed.

"So what else can you do?" Pobble asked.

Jed activated his rally spark and concentrated on the junk around them. *Coconut milk . . .* he said inside his head. From several miles away, his mind connected with a can of coconut milk. It ripped from the piles and soared toward him, then slapped against his open hand. He leaned over and handed the coconut milk to Kizer. "Here. Try this. I think it might be one of the only ingredients that could save that mess," he said with a wink.

Pobble clapped his hands and beamed at Jed.

Riggs released an admiring whistle.

Kizer didn't know whether to look completely terrified or utterly impressed.

Jed

As *Bessie* landed atop the dreadnought, Ryan stood waiting with Shay and Captain Bog.

Jed leaped from the side of the tugboat, startling everyone as he sailed through the air and landed gracefully beside them.

"You're not broken anymore!" Shay squeaked in delight.

His father wrapped him in a tight hug, and even Captain Bog gave him an admiring nod.

The rest of the tug crew ambled from their ship and reunited with their captain.

But Jed's happy grin faded almost as quickly as it had come when a dark voice returned to his mind.

"Rigger Hollow was a show of things to come if you do not return," Lyle said, with a wicked bite.

"Jed?" his dad said. "Are you all right?"

Jed told them of his connection with Lyle. "He won't stop until I go back."

"You can't do that," his dad said. "If you go back and he finds a way to use your sparks, he will be impossible to stop. Destroying cities would only be the beginning."

Jed nodded. "I know. What are we going to do?"

"I still have control of around seventy warships," Bog said. "I already sent ghostnoughts to follow his trail. If he moves against another city, I can send my legion to intercept. I'm not sure how long I can hold him off, but I can try."

"If you wage war, the iron and copper are just going to attack both of you," Ryan said. "They see this civil war as an opportunity to stop the dread once and for all."

"What other choice do we have?" Bog said.

Jed shot him a bemused look. "Going soft in your old age?" he asked.

"Shut up, kid," Bog scowled back.

"What about the gold city?" Jed said.

The others looked at him. "How do you know about that?" Ryan asked.

"Complicated story," Jed said. "How do *you* know about it?"

"A long time ago, your mother and I worked with the golds. They contacted us when they discovered that Lyle was going to reactivate you. They helped us find you. No one else knows where they are. They gave us that watch on your wrist as the only way to find them. But that was then. And I no longer have the spectacles needed to read the watch."

"I do," Riggs said.

The others looked at him.

"If you're going," Shay cut in, "I'm going with you. So you don't get lost again."

"That's a good idea," Ryan said. "Bog, do you have a cruiser they can take?"

"Lyle is hunting me," Jed said. "He probably has his own ghostnoughts lurking around the skies. If I take a ship, there's more of a chance that we'll get caught. I can fly there on my own using my sparks. I'll be harder to spot without a ship."

Shay grinned. "Perfect," she said. "And since I'll still be going with you, then you'll need to make me some wings."

. . .

"I've never made wings that can carry anything bigger than a tin can," Jed said dubiously, looking at Sprocket's wings. Shay's new wings were also cobbled together from junkyard parts. But Shay's set buckled on like a backpack and was patterned after a decidedly more elegant pair of wings—Alice's.

Thin hammered copper plates were fastened together with gears and wiring stretching back and forth. Jed infused the wings with energy from his spark the way he did with Sprocket's. A battery housing unit directed the power to the machine. Tiny whirring fans gave off a gentle hum. Shay danced in excitement when she saw them.

The crew met at the top deck, where Riggs examined Jed's watch.

"How far away does it say it is?" Shay asked.

"About three sunfalls," Riggs said, switching glasses.

"We'll hold off the dread," Bog said. "You two get there and bring help."

Jed's dad gripped both of his shoulders. "Don't get lost this time," he said.

Jed smiled. "Same to you."

Jed

Shay's eyes grew larger when her wings started to flutter. She lifted up and down, practicing. Before long, she was spinning, flipping, and squealing through the air.

Bog smiled fondly at her. "They suit you," he said.

"They do, don't they?" Shay said, twirling once in the air before landing delicately.

"Hold on," Bog said. "I want you to take something with you before you go." He left the deck and returned a few minutes later with a sack. "Here," he said, handing the sack to Shay. "Extra batteries. Plenty to keep your new wings running fresh. If you even start feeling a single battery limping behind," he said, holding up a scolding finger, "you go ahead and swap out the whole set. Clear? That boy's clunk engineering is questionable at best."

Shay grinned and wrapped him in a tight hug. "I love you, too," she said.

Jed watched as the gruff captain's face flushed a bright red.

Bog squeezed Shay with his burly arms before turning to Jed. "You let anything happen to my Shay," he said, eyes squinting with threat, "and I'll make sure your face makes mine look like it just won a beauty pageant award."

Unsure how to respond to that, Jed nodded uncomfortably.

"Shall we?" Shay said, her wings fluttering with excitement.

Bog lead them to the side of the ship, where Jed and Shay leaped into the open air.

Wind rushed past Jed's face, and his stomach pinched with excitement. As soon as he could sense the junk below, he mutinied himself diagonally away from it, soaring toward the bright sun.

Shay and Sprocket zipped along beside him. Shay barrel-rolled through the air, eyes giddy with her newfound freedom.

They flew all day, stopping only to replace her batteries as promised. When the sky turned a brilliant orange, they searched for a place to land.

Jed's sparks burned with heat. The long journey made them feel like tiny fireballs under his skin. The warmth filled every inch of him as if he had spent the day baking in an oven.

"How close?" Shay asked.

Jed checked his watch. "It says we're already here . . ." he said, confusion pulling at his tone.

The piles around them were barren. There was no city—floating or otherwise—in sight. The sun was nearly down, but there was still plenty of light to see that there was nothing here.

Shay frowned. "It's not a very big city, is it?"

This was supposed to be Lawnmower Mountain, but there wasn't a mountain anywhere—not for several sunfalls in any direction—let alone one made of lawn mowers.

Jed sat down and rested his forehead in his hands. *What's our backup plan?* he asked himself. Shay zipped around, unconcerned.

The final light of the sunset had vanished. Except . . . not entirely. A faint glint of yellow caught Jed's eye. It came from behind a kicked-in stereo system. He stared at it, waiting for it to disappear as the other light lacing the junk had. But it didn't. There was something beneath it.

"Hey," Jed called to Shay. "Come look at this."

Shay landed with a pout, and her eyes fixed on the spot of light.

"Do you see it?" Jed asked.

"Maybe it's a lemon," she said, licking her lips. "A sweet, sweet, lemon."

"I don't think it's a lemon," Jed said. "I think it's a light."

"Hmm. Could be. But a lemon sounds much better, don't you think?"

They inched closer to the sliver of light. Jed lifted his hands. He charged the light with mutiny and pushed. The gap widened. Jed mutinied harder. Junk squealed as it compressed and moved away from the light. Eventually, there was a gap big enough to crawl through.

"Ohh. It's pretty," Shay said as the light intensified. "Dig more! Dig more!"

Jed crawled into the tunnel and pushed again. Debris folded away, and Jed crept forward another few inches. With each kneeling step, he cleared more junk from his path. Shay scampered after him on hands and knees.

"It's below us," he said to her.

Jed charged the barrier of clutter to mutiny away. The tunnel opened underneath them. The yellow glow shot through the hole and lit the tunnel like a train steamrolling through. More junk broke free, sending Jed spiraling through the air.

Jed

A new world enveloped Jed—horizon to horizon—in yellow. He spun and tumbled down, down, down. *It's a sinkhole*, he thought. *A bubble popped. And I popped with it.*

Green and blue and gold filled his eyes. Far below him, grass and water stretched across the landscape. Overhead, a dome of brilliant yellow lights sparkled like a million tiny suns. Orchards speckled with yellow, red, and pink fruits dotted the view. Patches of the rich earthy fields surrounded a village of stone cottages. A mountain jutted unnaturally high in the distance. Green vines tangled through the mountain's surface, giving it a long-forgotten look. *There it is*, Jed thought. *Lawnmower Mountain.*

Jed fell so fast he nearly forgot he was falling. He tried to charge the mutiny spark before he collided with a grassy hill.

Nothing happened.

He had plenty of energy—that much he could feel. He tried the mutiny spark again, but it remained blocked. Jed's stomach pinched as he tried again and again without success. Panic built.

What if I shatter into a thousand bits of golden scrap?

Jed squeezed his eyes shut as the ground raced toward him.

A blinding pain shot through his body as he slammed into a patch of grass. If his body *had* shattered to bits, it couldn't have hurt worse than what he felt at this moment. The air was knocked out of him as he lay helplessly on the grass, wondering if his face had left a Jed-shaped indentation on the ground. Finally, once he was sure his limbs were still attached and in working order, he coughed and rolled onto his back.

From down here, the dome lights didn't look like lights at all. The sky glowed with a singular soft golden color. Metal wings fluttered over him as Shay twisted and flipped through the air. She landed softly beside him and took his hand, helping him to his feet.

"That must have been so much fun," she said. "If I were a brave mouse like you, I would've fallen all the way down and landed on my face, too." Her expression held a hint of jealousy at his "fun" plunge through the dome.

"Oh, hello," Shay said, waving to something behind Jed.

He turned around and saw a group of figures standing in silence beside a stone water well. Some of them had half-filled pails; others waited with empty ones. The figures were gold. All of them. Not an ounce of skin on them. They were beautiful. Fine rods of gold connected to golden hinges. Golden gears spinning behind golden grates.

They stared at Shay and him, motionless.

"Um, hi?" Jed said, waving with Shay.

"Humans!" one of them yelled.

As if they just now saw the two for the first time, the golds near the water well ran frantically. Several of them collided into one another and fell. Others tripped over the fallen golds. They looked a bit like an amateur circus troupe as they bumbled over one another to get away.

"Humans!"

"Humans!"

"Humans!" they yelled. "Call for the sentinels!"

"Wait," Jed called after them. "No, I'm not—"

Metallic sirens clanged. Jed spun around. A small company of three armored soldiers hustled toward him. The man in the middle looked to be at least a head shorter then Jed, the man on the left was about his size, and the woman on the right dwarfed the other two with her towering height. They were clad in ill-fitting plates of silver armor.

"Halt in the name of the queen!" the short one shouted.

"They look mad," Shay whispered to Jed.

"Wait," Jed said, holding out his hands. "We're not here to hurt anyone."

"Fire!" the middle soldier bellowed to the other two.

The awkward trio heaved shatterkegs nearly as big as

themselves. They fired. Jed winced, awaiting the impact. Explosions shook the ground around them, but none of the shots hit him or Shay. The force of the mobile shatterkegs spun two of the soldiers around and knocked the third on her back. Before Jed could call out again, they were back on their feet and firing another volley.

The soldiers' eyes were wide with fear. Their arms shook as if they'd never battled before.

"Fire!" the shortest one shouted again. This round was worse than the first. All three shots flew over Jed's head and struck grassy patches in the distance.

"Stop," Jed called. "We're not here to attack."

But the nervous soldiers weren't listening. Their arms rattled with panic as they continued to fire round after round, frantic but completely inept. The closer they drew, the worse their aim became.

They ran toward Jed and Shay, launching another volley. One of them fired a shot before he'd even had a chance to lift the shatterkeg. Aimed at the ground, the weapon blasted the terrified gold into the air.

The soldiers scrambled closer. They struggled to aim and fire their shatterkegs. Finally, one of the shots clipped Jed's shoulder. The impact sent him spinning to the ground. The soldiers raised their shatterkegs at Jed; their eyes landed on his shoulder.

They froze.

"Gold," the tall woman whispered.

"Yes," Jed said quickly, before they had a chance to fire

again. "That's what I've been trying to tell you. We're not humans. We're like you."

The gold woman squinted at Jed. "Why are you wearing that human suit?" she asked. "We thought you were one of them."

"Human suits are terribly comfortable," Shay said, pinching the skin on her arm. "So squishy and soft. Like a snuggly little blanket."

"We didn't grow up here," Jed added. "I lived my whole life somewhere else. With humans."

"But how?" the short one asked.

"They're roguespawn," the woman whispered.

Shay folded her arms angrily. "That doesn't sound very nice."

"Roguespawn?" Jed asked. "What's roguespawn?"

"Who's your tinkerer?" the middle one asked.

"I don't know what that means," Jed said.

"Who put you both together?"

Jed swallowed hard. *Oh.* That's what they meant by roguespawn.

Lyle, the rogue gold.

"A very mean mouse," Shay said.

"His name," Jed began, hesitation thick in his tone, "is Lyle." The three nodded and whispered conspiratorially to one another softly enough that Jed couldn't hear. "But we're nothing like him," Jed continued. "He captured me, and I escaped from him."

"What about her?"

Shay considered herself. "I'm questionable," she said.

The three huddled together and chattered. After a moment, they faced him again. "We have determined," the short one said confidently, "that we don't know what to do with you."

The others nodded in agreement.

"Okay?" Jed said.

"You are quite possibly a danger," the one on the left said. "So, we will take you to the queen. Immediately. She will know what to do with you."

"After lunch," the shortest one whispered to him.

"After lunch," the one on the left amended. He lifted his shatterkeg up, resting its bulk on his shoulder. It fired inadvertently, blasting him forward.

"Yes!" Shay shrieked. "I do love lunch."

Jed looked up at the artificial sky. *Lunch?* It was nighttime outside of the dome, but it looked like midday under the golden sky. He wondered if the golds beneath the junk ever knew when it was day or night.

He turned back to the golds. "Calliope, right?" Jed asked. "Is she still your queen?"

"How do you know Calliope?" the one on the right asked, raising her shatterkeg threateningly.

"I saw some of Lyle's memories. I saw what the humans did to you. I'm here to help. Or, ask for *your* help *against* Lyle."

"I'm afraid this conversation is over," the one in the middle said. "At least until we've eaten lunch."

"Shelpin's making kebabs in the town square again," the one on the right said.

"Ooo, I love her kebabs."

"Best kebabs in the city," the one on the left said.

"What do you think she uses to season her mushrooms?" the one in the middle asked, turning around and walking toward the town square.

"I bet garlic powder, onion, and black pepper," the left one said, following him, "but you know Shelpin. She never tells."

The three soldiers completely forgot about Jed and Shay as they walked off, shatterkegs slung casually over their shoulders. When they'd traveled a few dozen paces, the one in the middle spun around, frantic. "The prisoners!" he shouted. "They've escaped! Where did they—" His eyes stopped on Jed and his tense shoulders relaxed. "Tricky little roguespawn. Trying to distract us. Tempting us with delicious kebabs."

"Seriously?" Jed said. "I'm pretty sure you tempted yourself."

"One more word out of you," the soldier said, "and you won't be getting a third helping! Do I make myself clear?" The short gold put on his best stern face.

"Crystal clear," Jed said.

The gold nodded curtly. "Then follow behind, prisoners. Or are prisoners supposed to go first?"

"How about we walk beside you?" Shay suggested.

The three soldiers considered it and then nodded.

"I'm Hift, by the way," the shortest said.

"Taskon," the one on the left said, waving.

"And I'm Murjen," the tall woman said.

"It's nice to meet all of you," Shay said. "I'm Shay. He's Jed. Now let's go eat!"

They followed a cobblestone road that weaved through apple orchards, small garden plots of vegetables, and two ponds bustling with orange, red, and violet fish.

The road led into a small collection of cottages. The scent of cooking wafted from everywhere. Meats, breads, and vegetables. Jed's stomach tickled with delight, and he tried to remind himself that his mission here was critical. But the smell of food . . . he had never felt more gold.

"Is there a celebration going on?" he asked.

"Yep," Taskon said. "Lunch."

The townspeople began emerging from their cottages with carefully packaged dishes in small baskets.

"Everyone eats lunch together?" Jed asked.

Murjen nodded. "Of course. Otherwise we'd have to go door to door to sample the new recipes. That would be ridiculous." They all chuckled.

"You mean you eat all the meals together?"

"Doesn't everybody?" Hift said.

"I like this place," Shay whispered to Jed.

One of the golds carrying a basket of freshly baked rolls turned and saw Jed and Shay. She shrieked, tossing the basket into the air. Rolls tumbled to the ground. "Humans!"

Hift held up his hand. "It's all right, everyone. We've got things under control." He put his fists on his hips and puffed out his chest proudly. "These prisoners won't be any trouble." He turned to Jed and Shay. "Will you?"

He said the last words with a bit of worry in his tone.

"We're good mice," Shay said.

The townspeople stared at them.

"Hi. I'm also not a human," Jed said. "Just raised by them. Lived with them. Thought I *was* one until recently. You know, typical childhood stuff."

"I'm hungry!" Shay said.

One by one, the townspeople began attending their dishes again. They continued, however, to glance at the prisoners with worried looks, as if one of them might suddenly attack.

"Don't worry, we're taking him to the queen," Murjen added.

"But not until after lunch, right?" one of the townspeople spoke up. "Shelpin's cooking kebabs again!"

"Of course, not until after lunch," Murjen said.

Hift marched them to a woman working at a portable grill. "Shelpin," he said, "this is Jed and Shay. Our roguespawn prisoners." Hift stood up straighter and puffed out his chest in pride.

"Oh, how exciting," Shelpin said, skewering some pieces of meat, peppers, and mushrooms. "How do you do, roguespawns?" she asked.

"Radiantly," Shay said, extending her hand.

Shelpin shook it and then shook Jed's. "I'm Shelpin. Care for a kebab?" She lifted one of the cooked skewers from the grill. Delicate black char lines streaked the meat and vegetables.

Jed took the skewer and bit off one of the mushrooms. "These are incredible," he said to her. She smiled proudly. Jed thought for a moment. "Let's see. I'm guessing you used thyme, lemon zest, sage, and . . . is that a hint of porcini sea salt?"

Shelpin's mouth dropped open. "How did you—"

"It's absolutely wonderful," Jed said. "Just perfect."

Shelpin huffed, turning to Hift. "I don't like your roguespawn anymore."

Taskon patted Jed on the back. "Well done, roguespawn! Well done."

A bell echoed through the town square.

"Lunchtime!" Hift said, rubbing his hands in delighted anticipation.

Hundreds of golds gathered in the square, empty plates at the ready. They wandered from stove to stove, dishing up vegetables, potatoes, pastas, cheeses, breads, and meats.

Hift gave Jed and Shay each an oversize plate. "For our new guests," he said.

"You mean prisoners?" Jed asked.

Hift's brow scrunched together. "Oh, right." He snatched the oversize plates from them and gave them regular plates instead. "There. Now, no escaping. Or doing other things you shouldn't be doing."

"Like making faces like this?" Shay asked, sticking out her tongue and squinching her face into a wrinkled knot.

Hift nodded. "Exactly."

For the next hour, everyone in the town square stuffed themselves with jelly-covered pastries, meats with gravy, and fruits with sweet cream. Jed picked at the food anxiously, waiting for lunch to end.

Finally, he approached Hift. "Shouldn't you be taking us to the queen?" Jed asked. "We really need to speak with her."

"But lunch isn't over yet," Hift said, confused.

"How long does lunch last?"

Hift looked around in surprise. "Until all the food is gone, of course."

The food wasn't even close to gone.

"We really need to see the queen. Can't you just take us there and come back?"

Hift sighed. "Prisoners are more work than I thought they'd be," he grumbled, rolling his eyes at Jed. "Fine. Get your roguespawn accomplice and follow me."

. . .

The "palace" turned out to be no more than another cottage with a signpost in the grass that read: PALACE.

"Why isn't Queen Calliope with the rest of the town for lunch?" Jed asked.

"She only comes out every third lunch. Apparently, she's too busy," Hift said.

"Sounds like a terrible job to me," Murjen piped up. "Remind me never to be queen."

Hift and Takson nodded in agreement. Jed stifled the urge to push them forward.

The five of them walked to the door, and Hift knocked.

"Come in," a gentle voice called.

The group entered the cottage. Books, papers, files, scrolls, and folders lined the walls. Floor to ceiling. Corner to corner. The home was one giant bookshelf. A woman sat in a comfortable-looking chair in the corner of the room. Jed immediately recognized her from Lyle's memories. Seeing her through his own eyes, though, he marveled—the same way Lyle had—at her intricate gearwork. The machinery was so fine that it even dimpled as she moved, the very way skin did.

Queen Calliope set a large tome on the coffee table beside her chair and stood. Her gaze traveled from Jed over to Shay, and then to the three guards. "What are *humans* doing here, Sergeant Hift?"

Hift quickly pointed to Jed's burned shoulder. "They are not humans," he said. "They only *look* like them because they're wearing their skins."

An uncomfortable thought suddenly prickled Jed's mind. Where *had* he gotten his skin?

"Who are you?" Calliope asked Jed and Shay.

"We escaped from Lyle," Jed said.

She studied him, scanning his face. "You're *him*," she said. "The one that Lyle worked on for so many years. I can see it in your bones."

Jed nodded uncomfortably.

"Are you really a queen?" Shay broke in excitedly. "I've always wanted to meet a queen."

Calliope nodded slowly, then her eyes filled with pity. "Yes, I am. And you must be Lyle's other. Yes?"

"Shay," she introduced herself confidently.

Calliope assessed her. "You recovered quite nicely after Lyle's experiments."

Shay looked as if she didn't quite know how to respond.

"Oh, I'm sorry," Calliope said, gliding forward and resting a hand on Shay's shoulder. "I didn't mean anything by that. You seem like a lovely girl. Truly."

Shay's face brightened again with a smile. "I'm quite lovely," Shay agreed.

"Why have you both come?" the queen asked, directing the question at them both but glancing at Jed as she asked it.

"We need your help," Jed said. "Lyle is destroying sky cities. He's waging war against the humans with his dread army."

Calliope shook her head. "We came here to escape war. We can't help you. Our people aren't built for conflict," she said. She glanced at the three guards, who were surreptitiously rubbing their stomachs and whispering about the food they were upset they weren't eating.

"Taskon, Hift, and Murjen are among the best soldiers we have," the queen concluded. She turned to them, sudden apology in her eyes. "I mean that in the kindest way possible.

"It's why we were slaughtered all those years ago," she continued. "Most of these golds don't even know of the dangers out there. I only do because I've lived through them. We are a peaceful people. We cook, we paint, and we invent. Others take advantage of that. They steal from us and kill what's left. We can't help you. We wouldn't be of any use. Besides, even if we could help, I would still refuse. I want no part in the world above the junk. We do not belong there."

"But he's killing the humans. Destroying entire cities," Jed said, trying to make her understand the urgency of the situation.

"The more humans he kills, the fewer humans there are to kill and steal from us."

"Do you think he will really stop once he's done with the humans? I've been inside his memories. He blames you for everything bad that's happened to him. He wants revenge."

"What are you really asking for?" Calliope asked. "You've clearly seen our military ineptitude."

"Lawnmower Mountain," Jed said. "Does it still work?"

Calliope's face darkened. "It's never really worked. Not for more than three hundred hours."

"Tash," Jed said. "Right? Lyle said that Tash's design would only work for two to four weeks."

Calliope nodded slowly. "Lyle was unfortunately right. Tash activated the mountain long enough to help us escape and to dig our new home here, where no one would find us again. The mountain died soon after. And it seems our goal of staying hidden has also failed. You did find us."

"I saw Lyle's memories. I was built to activate the mountain."

Calliope shook her head. "That man tried to use you to make that mountain work for many years, and he never succeeded. And then . . . something terrible happened to Lyle. Perhaps it was his obsession, but I believe it was something more."

"The last experiment," Jed said. "When he plugged himself into the mountain?"

Calliope nodded. "It broke him somehow . . . turned him into a monster."

"I'm not Lyle," Jed said. "Please, let *me* try."

"No," she answered.

"What do you have to lose?"

"You mean, besides our entire civilization?"

"What about the fail-safe?" Jed begged. "It will protect you."

"What fail-safe?"

"The fail-safe that destroys the mountain," Jed said. "In case someone does something with the mountain and you need to stop them. You can activate the lawn mowers, and the mountain will wreck itself."

"But you could still destroy us," she said, shaking her head. "No. I think it is better to lock you up instead."

"What? Are you kidding me?" Jed demanded.

"Jokes are not one of my strengths," she said. "And don't try to use your sparks. We have dampeners placed throughout the city to protect us against Lyle and his weapons."

"I'm not a weapon," Jed said. "I'm a gold. Like you. And you're going to lock me up?"

She sighed. "Unfortunately, yes. It is the best course of action. I must keep my people safe."

"Taskon, Hift, and Murjen?" the queen said, turning to the three soldiers. "Please escort these two to the dungeon in Ricklebottom's cellar."

"Don't do this," Jed begged. "I need your help. The humans need your help. The whole world needs your help."

"We can do nothing," the queen said with finality. She nodded at the guards, wordlessly ordering them to take Jed away.

"You heard the queen," Hift said, popping to attention. "Orders are orders."

Jed looked at the three guards. He and Shay could resist them—it wouldn't even be hard—but it didn't matter. With the dampeners, this place was a prison. Besides, they needed Lawnmower Mountain. Bog was counting on them to get to it. Lyle's fleet would soon be attacking more innocent town-ships, so Jed would just have to stay here until he had it.

Hift prodded them out of the palace. "Let's get you both to the dungeon, yes?" he said.

"What about lunch?" Jed asked. "You don't want to miss the end, do you? You didn't even get to try everything, and there was so much food left."

Murjen leaned in to her compatriots. "He's got a solid point," she murmured.

"What's the harm in waiting until after lunch to imprison them?" Taskon asked.

"Very true," Hift said. "Lunch it is!"

The three guards turned around and scrambled toward the

town square, leaving Shay and Jed unguarded, forgotten, and alone. Again.

Shay turned to follow, licking her lips in anticipation. Jed grabbed her arm. She turned and frowned at him, taking a moment to catch on. "We're not going back for food, are we?" she said with a pout.

"Nope. Sorry."

"Not even a teensy squeak of a nibble?" she asked, hopefully.

"I can't activate my sparks," Jed said. "That means I can't fly. I'm stuck here until I can find a way to get the dampeners off-line. You need to fly out of the dome and get back to the tug. Tell them I'm still working on activating the mountain."

Shay rolled her eyes. "Fine," she said. "But can I at least take a kebab?"

Jed

Once Shay was gone, Jed headed back into the town square to gather his "guards."

He tapped Hift on the shoulder. The short man had a kebab nearly to his open mouth. He paused and sighed as he noticed Jed.

"Right . . ." he mumbled. "Prison, yes?"

"If you wouldn't mind," Jed said with a nod.

Hift released an exaggerated sigh as he begrudgingly set down his kebab and brushed cake crumbs from his trousers. "Follow me, I suppose. Murjen! Taskon!" he called.

The other two guards glared at Jed but put down their plates and joined Hift to escort the prisoner. None of them even seemed to notice that Shay was missing.

The prison was a basement under a basement, and it was much more secure than Jed had expected—or wanted. The stone walls were thick, and the door was made from heavy wood and straps of steel.

"Happy?" Hift said as he shut the door and locked it.

Sprocket rolled out from his backpack. "Zzztuck," she said, looking around the dimly lit room.

Jed sighed. "Quite stuck," he agreed. "But don't worry, we'll be *un*stuck from here soon."

. . .

Within four hours, the latch lifted on his prison door.

Time for midevening tea and cakes.

Murjen carried a tray decorated neatly with a porcelain teacup and freshly baked biscuits. "Good evening," she said sheepishly, holding the tray up so Jed could see it. A small daisy sat in a miniature vase as an adornment to the snack.

Every meal the golds brought him looked, smelled, and tasted like it had been made by a four-star chef: broiled flat-iron steak, maple-glazed salmon with pineapple salsa, and spice-rubbed beef tenderloins with chimichurri. He ate better in this prison than he did at almost any other time in his life, and more often. They brought meals seven times the first day.

"We don't get a lot of prisoners," Hift had explained apologetically at the time. "Do prisoners prefer nine meals a day? What, with all that sitting around and having nothing else to do but eat? Sounds dreadful."

He'd been stuck in this prison for only two full days, but they'd already given him a week's worth of food.

Jed's mind snapped back to Murjen. "Um ... is there ... uh ... anything else I can do for you?" she asked, setting down the tea and biscuits and looking sorrowfully at the dank surroundings.

"Besides letting me go?" Jed asked.

"Yeah, besides that."

"I'm fine," Jed grumped.

Murjen reached down to the tray and adjusted the daisy, then nodded to herself in approval as he looked at the tray. "I'll be back in an hour for supper," she said, her voice breaking with the prospect. "I'll check on the cooking now! Prisoners should never be subjected to burned duck confit."

Alone again, Jed looked at Sprocket. "Do you think Shay made it back?"

"Yezzz."

He'd already scoured the walls of the prison for any loose stones that he might pull away to tunnel free, but the wall was solid. Golds might not be good at taking prisoners, but they were good at keeping them.

"We have to get out of this basement," he whispered to Sprocket. "I have an idea, but I'm going to need your help."

"Helllp."

At supper, Murjen brought in a plate covered by a large silver serving dish. "Perfectly roasted duck confit," she said, whipping the cover off the food with a flourish. "Enjoy."

When Jed finished eating, he hid Sprocket on the finished

tray to be taken for washing. Now he just had to wait. That night, once the town was stuffed and sleeping, Sprocket returned and lifted the prison's latch bar. Together, Jed and his faithful tin can snuck out of the root cellar and into the open town square.

Sprocket sped alongside Jed, fluttering happily in the still air. The dome lights had dimmed to pinpricks of white light, like stars. Violet battery bugs—much like the green one he'd purchased in Lunkway for Alice—hovered in distant orchards and gardens.

Jed walked toward Lawnmower Mountain. Dirt and rocks crunched under his steps until he reached a field of grass. The soft earth made him want to take off his shoes and walk in the cool lawn the way he used to at his home beyond the fringe. The mountain grew taller the closer Jed got to it. Flowering vines weaved through the heaps of lawn mowers.

Jed walked around the base until he spotted what looked like the mouth of a cave. Vines covered the dark opening like prison bars. He peered inside but couldn't see anything within the black depths.

He needed light. A trip back to the village was too risky, but the memory of Lyle using the key on Jed—the key that allowed him to remove his skin—jumped into his mind. Could he do it without the key? Could he take off his skin? He closed his eyes, remembering how it had felt. The sound of the clicking key. The movement of the gears inside his chest. The sensation against his skin was gone. The gentle breeze. The slight chill of night. Gone.

Jed's skin slouched around his gold. He removed it entirely. The thousands of sparks inside of him shined with a light of their own. Spark light pierced the blackness of the cave. Jagged shapes ran along a corridor that extended into the heart of the mountain.

Jed pried through the vines that grew across the opening, and squeezed into the cavern. His brilliant sparks glowed brighter in the total darkness of the cave, and the silence of the night was broken only by the sound of his light footsteps on the ground.

Jed walked until he could barely see the entrance, Sprocket still dancing beside him. He crept farther in until a chamber opened. It domed overhead as far as he could see. In the center of the chamber was a ladder, too tall for Jed to see its end.

"Well," he said to Sprocket, who fluttered nearer and then perched on his shoulder. "Shall we?"

Jed

"Toppp," Sprocket buzzed.

"Finally," Jed said. "If we ever get out of this hole in the ground and make it back aboard Bog's tugboat, I want you to tell Kizer—straight to his grim face—that I can climb a clunk ladder. Okay?"

"Clllunk faaace," Sprocket said. "Ladderrr."

"Exactly."

The ladder stretched to an empty room at the hollow peak of the mountain. A gap in one wall overlooked the city. Jed could see everything: the starry sky, the town square, and even the root cellar from which he'd escaped. More purple battery bugs filled the dome, spreading over the grass like a violet mist.

But there was nothing inside the room—no control panel, no levers or gears or buttons. Only a single cable dangled from the ceiling.

Turning away from the outside world, he approached the cable warily. Loose, exposed wires snarled from its end. Jed looked from the cable to his chest.

Sprocket buzzed.

"Yeah, I don't think I'm putting that in me just yet. We need to shut down those dampeners first," Jed said to Sprocket.

She sputtered in agreement.

. . .

Jed was back in his prison before sunup. Sprocket was tucked in a corner nearby, looking as innocent as a cherry pie filling can can look. They repeated the routine the next night; Sprocket opened the prison door, and Jed studied the mountain or searched for the spark inhibitors.

There was a little problem with that second task, though: Jed didn't have the faintest idea what a spark inhibitor looked like.

On the third night, Jed was sitting at the mountain base, wondering what he should do. Lyle would be on the hunt for him. They were safe now, but how long could that last? He needed to activate the mountain.

"What's your secret?" he whispered to its forbidding shape.

Sprocket fluttered about in the grass. She weaved around

flowers, occasionally hunching over them as if smelling the petals. The longer Jed sat, the bolder she grew in exploring the space around them.

Jed lay back on the cool ground, interlocking his hands behind his head. "What do you think, Sprocket?"

He waited for an answer.

"Sprocket?" he said again.

Nothing.

He sat up. She wasn't beside him.

"Sprocket?" he called a third time.

A light buzzing noise came from the side of the mountain.

Jed hopped up and walked after her, following the sound of her wings. A dim purple light pulsed in the distance. Jed smiled to himself. She had been chasing a battery bug. As he drew closer, he could see her awkward shape trying to match the rise and fall of the battery bug's movement.

"Prrretty," Sprocket buzzed. "Zzzpark!"

"Yeah, it's kind of like a spark," Jed said, jogging to catch her.

He walked with her around the base of the mountain as she delightedly chased the battery bug. They walked nearly halfway around the mountain before Jed stopped. "We should head back," he called softly to Sprocket. "Before the sun—I guess the lights—come up."

"Light! Light! Light!" Sprocket chanted.

"Exactly," Jed said.

"Seee!" Sprocket said, "Seee!"

She raced ahead, passing the battery bug.

"Wait!" Jed called, running after her. Then he saw it, too—a red dot blinked in the distance. He squinted. "What *is* that?"

"Light!" Sprocket said as she reached it. She flew like a tornado around the red dot.

Jed finally caught up and found a simple post sticking out of the ground. At the top of the post was a big red button. Next to the button was a sign: DO NOT PUSH.

A chill trickled from the back of Jed's neck down to his toes.

"Mom. Dad," he whispered in the cool night air, thinking back to the letter they'd left him so long ago. "I hope you're right."

And then he pushed the button.

Jed

Color bled through the sky as the dome lights changed from black to crimson. A siren wailed three times and then fell silent.

Sweat beaded in Jed's palm. *What have I done?*

His vision flickered, and a voice entered his mind.

"Jed?" Shay's voice said inside his head. "Are you there? I can feel you again. What happened? You were gone, but now you're back. Like a super-secret magic mouse! You are back, aren't you?"

"Yes, I'm here," he answered in his mind. "I think Sprocket found the dampener controls."

"Good. We're close," Shay continued. "But there's a teensy, tinesy, itty, bitty nibblet of a problem."

As if Jed could hear what Shay could hear, background noises echoed through their link. Sizzling wires . . . distant warning sirens . . . shatterfire.

"Shay?" Jed panicked. "What's going on?"

"Have you ever heard squeak of I.C.C.A.D.?"

Jed thought back to the tavern in Lunkway. "The Iron Copper Coalition Against Dread," he said in his mind. "What about them? Are they following you?"

"Well . . . we had to sneak through copper mouse skies," Shay said. "But copper mice didn't think it was very funny to see so many scritchnoughts. So, they called *aaalllll* of their friends, and now they're exploding us. Boom! Bang! Kasplooot! But don't worry, we're not exploding them back. Well . . . not *too* many of them. Ugly Mouse said, 'Don't stay and fight; go, go, go to save Jed!' Ooo . . . are you a mountain yet?"

"Are you going to be all right?" Jed asked.

"Probably. Ugly Mouse says that—"

Lyle's whispering voice snuffed out Shay's. "Jed, Jed, Jed . . . It's so good to feel your presence again. I'm quite hurt that you left without saying good-bye. Not even a single word. That was entirely inconsiderate. I thought you'd been killed or kidnapped a *second* time. I withdrew my entire fleet to look for you. I launched ghostnoughts in every direction. It was as if you had just vanished.

"I thought you were gone forever. But then there was that junkstorm. You're not the only one with relics that can predict junkstorm locations. . . . When your storm blew in out of nowhere with no warning on my radar, I knew you were behind it. So, I waited at the edge of town for days. Then I saw your old tugboat and I found your signal—your scent.

"I followed, but you disappeared yet *again*. Your signal evaporated completely this time. Until now. I take it you found those bumbling golden fools?"

"Leave them alone," Jed said angrily.

"They deserve it."

"I watched the memory. You abandoned *them*. Not the other way around."

"I *saved* them from the coppers and irons. And then the golds hid—even from me. I've spent a century searching. You find them in one day."

"They don't want to be found. They're not hurting anybody. Just leave them alone."

"I will leave them alone . . . once the hiding place they've built is their gravesite. Then I will leave them alone."

Shay's voice seeped back. "And that's why I think Ugly Mouse is always so grumpy," she said. "He just needs a big, tight, mouse squeeze."

"Shay," Jed said. "You need to get here soon. Lyle knows where I am. He's coming."

"Hmm. That's going to be a whole lot of mice squeezed in one little burrow. A whole lot, indeed."

"Goldzzz," Sprocket buzzed.

Jed looked up. A troop of guards rushed around the mountain toward them.

"Shay. I have to go. Get here as soon as you can."

"Quick as a whisker!"

"What have you done?" Queen Calliope called out. "You've shut down our *only* defenses!"

Hift, Murjen, and Taskon reached Jed first. Calliope trailed close behind. "Get the dampeners online immediately."

A technician stepped forward and knelt before the post. He opened a panel in its middle and fiddled with the wires until the crimson sky retuned to its bright, daytime gold. "I can reset the dampener cells," he said, "but it will take at least four hours to warm up."

"We're defenseless until then?" she asked.

The technician nodded.

"Get him back to his cell," Calliope snapped, stabbing a finger in Jed's direction.

"No," Jed said. "Lyle is coming. I need to be out here—I have to be ready for him."

"You've put our entire city in peril," Calliope said. "Guards, take him."

Jed aimed a hand at Hift. "You don't want to do this. I'm not your enemy."

"Take him now!" Calliope shouted.

The three guards stepped forward. Jed charged them with mutiny against the ground underneath their feet. They floated a few feet in the air.

"Ah!" Hift shouted. "What's going—"

Boom!

Hift accidently fired his shatterkeg. The force of the blast launched him toward Lawnmower Mountain, where he smacked its vine-covered surface and tumbled to the ground with a confused "Ouch!"

"That was him, not me." Jed cringed. He turned to Calliope. "Let me help you. *Please*. I can do this."

The anger in her eyes faded to despair. "He'll kill us all," she said in a softer tone. "He burns with so much hatred."

"I won't let him."

"He has an army. Legions of undead that will tear all of us into scrap."

"And we have an entire mountain," Jed said.

Before Calliope could respond, Lyle's slippery voice crawled into Jed's ears. "Ahh. It's good to be home."

An explosion rattled the earth. The dome lights flicked out. Bits of debris trickled down into the gold city.

"He's here," Calliope said.

Jed nodded. Two more explosions rumbled in the dome. The hole where Jed had entered erupted in flames. Chunks of metal rained down. The hole grew wider and wider until it was enormous—a black disk in a golden sky.

The explosions ceased and the flames fizzled.

Everything was still for a moment.

Then, as the smoke dissipated, a ship floated through the hole.

"Dreadnought," Jed said.

Another dreadnought descended after it. Then a third and a fourth. Soon, a dozen ships floated above the peaceful orchards, ponds, fields, and gardens. They flew slowly, hauntingly. Their engines coughed black trails of smoke as they clustered into battle formation.

Calliope turned to Jed. "Do it."

Jed turned and ran. His feet pounded the earth with purpose.

"Faster," he said, rounding the base of the mountain and rallying to the top.

Jed

"Shay?" Jed called out in his mind.

"Jed," Shay answered. "We're two squeaks away. We see Lyle's mousenoughts. They're scampering inside the gold burrow."

Jed nodded to himself. "I know. I'm going to try to stop them."

"Be careful. Or don't be careful, and smash up their boats. But don't die. We'll be there soon, unless we get squashed."

Jed heard Captain Bog's voice in the background. "Shay! Stop jabbering and help me get this pulse beam online!"

"Gotta go," Shay said. Her voice faded and disappeared.

Jed faced the thick cable hanging from the ceiling. "I can do this."

He walked toward the cable, pulled off his shirt, and plugged the cable into his chest. A waterfall of energy gushed from the end of the cable, flooding every capacitor in his body with raw power. His sparks drank it in.

Jed felt for the lawn mowers. They appeared inside his mind one at a time, then dozens at a time, then hundreds, and then thousands, until he could feel them all—each lawn mower, a wave in an ocean of power.

Jed focused on the closest dreadnought. "Go," he commanded.

A lawn mower sailed across the sky. It tumbled end over end as it flew toward the ship. The mower snapped against the ship's hull. Jed infused the mower with life. Its blades ground into the side of the dreadnought, sending bits of wood and metal spraying everywhere as it crawled back and forth, chomping everything in its path.

Jed felt for more mowers, this time charging a hundred at once.

"Start," he commanded.

Their motors chugged to life, coughing exhaust and sending tiny fumes of black smoke out from the mountain simultaneously.

"Go."

The mowers swarmed toward the dreadnought, too, joining the first mower in tearing bits and scrap from its body.

Jed hurled hundreds more at the ship until, finally, the lawn mowers chewed the engines to pieces and the dreadnought sank from the sky.

Jed focused on a second dreadnought. He flared his rally sparks and anchored the ship to the drifting, dead dreadnought. Jed rallied the two ships toward each other until they slammed together. Metal crunched against metal and rained down.

"You can't stop them all," Lyle's voice whispered in his head. "I have enough ships to fill this little warren to its brim."

"Leave!" Jed yelled back.

"Certainly," Lyle said. "I'll leave as quickly as I came . . . if you come with me."

"I'm not going anywhere with you," Jed said.

"Then watch your home world burn."

Jed's throat felt thick and lumpy. There was something so innocent about this place. Something so perfect. He couldn't watch the golds be obliterated by Lyle, could he? He thought of Hift, Murjen, and Taskon. Of Shelpin and her kebabs. Of Calliope. But what choice was there?

If Jed went with Lyle, humans would die. If Jed stayed, then golds would die.

"We're here!" Shay squeaked in his mind.

Shatterbricks plummeted through the opening in the dome, slamming into Lyle's dreadnoughts. The ships inside the dome turned slowly in the sky, pivoting to face the new threat.

"Tell your friends to leave," Lyle said, "or I will lay waste to this pathetic town!"

Fear welled inside Jed's throat. He pictured charcoaled ruins in place of the lively lunchtime square. He looked at the gardens and orchards and lakes. All the glorious color, life, and smiles in this happy little hideaway . . . *gone*. Obliterated. Dead.

The outline of a ship at the top of the dome caught his eye. *Bessie*, the tugboat, breached the opening and entered the fray. The boat was a speck among giants, yet it launched shatterfire in a furious attack against the nearest dreadnought. The shatterkeg shells made dents in the dreadnought hulls. It was a suicide mission, but the tug crew fought all the same. Resolve, confidence, and hope swelled inside Jed. If Shay, Bog, and the rest of the crew could be so brave, Jed could be, too.

"I'm not a puppet," he called to Lyle. "Not yours or anyone else's. Now get out of here or I'll smash your ships to bits, one at a time."

"Keep throwing your cute lawn mowers at us, little one," Lyle taunted.

Fury bubbled inside Jed. He concentrated, connecting the hundreds of thousands of waves inside his ocean of power.

Shay

Bog squinted at the mountain. "What is going on?"

The mountain was changing. It swelled and shrank, twisted and stretched. Two long arms took shape on its side. Then two wide legs split apart at the base. The lawn mowers shifted and then settled into the shape of a—

"Mountain monster!" Shay squeaked. "Right there, right there!" She pointed over and over and over at the mountain. "Do you see it? Do you see it? Right there!"

Captain Bog's eyes were unmoving. His mouth gaped at the monster. "Shay. An entire mountain made completely out of *lawn mowers* is walking toward us. Yes. I see it."

She scowled at him. "Well you don't have to ruin all the fun by being mean," she said.

"The . . . *fun*? What about that says *fun* to you? The part where we get crushed by a hundred thousand tons of lawn mowers, or the part about a scrap clunking killer *mountain* that is alive and walking around?"

"Yes!" Shay said, delighted. "That part. Definitely that part."

"Well, enjoy it while we're alive, I suppose."

"Silly mouse," she said. "It's Jed. He wouldn't hurt us."

Outside, the mountain monster lifted one of its massive arms and brought it down onto one of the approaching war-noughts. The ship exploded into scrap.

"Right," Bog said. "Totally harmless."

"Don't worry," Shay said. "He's on our side."

"I sure hope so. Because no one's fighting that thing and coming out in one piece. Though . . . I'm not sure *any* of us are going to make it out of here in one piece."

"Our scritchmites will protect us," Shay said.

Bog sighed. "That's the problem: Looks like Lyle's got twice as many scritchmites as we do."

He isn't wrong, Shay thought to herself as they descended deeper into the dome. Lyle had brought every last boat, while most of Bog's boats were still trying to protect the human cities—which happened to also be trying to kill them.

"Do you remember the last time we played checkers?" Shay asked Bog. He nodded slowly, studying the scene before them. "Let's be brave like my last, lonely, little mouseling piece. No matter what, okay?"

Bog gave her his full attention and smiled. "Deal," he said. "We'll be brave together."

Shay and Bog turned back toward the bridge viewports. Bog's dreadnoughts poured through the opening around them into a sky filled with enemies. They looked like swarms of flies, spitting fire at one another.

Fire-spitting flies . . . Shay thought to herself. Now *that* was something to be afraid of.

"Circuit," Bog called to one of the helmscritches. He was a silly looking dread with big headphones drilled straight into his ears. Shay wondered if he even *had* ears underneath the headphones at all, or if the headphones *were* his ears.

"Captain?" the obedient scritch responded.

"Do we have any music on this ship?" Bog asked.

"I gots my very own record player down in my bunk," Circuit said proudly.

"Bring it up here, will you? If we're going to get shot down today, this time I'd like to do it with a bit of music. Last time was terribly irritating waiting to crash into the barge on a ship where the only sounds were thousands of shrieking dread."

Circuit scrambled out of his station and hurried from the bridge. He was back before Shay could even squeak, carrying a boxy record player nearly as big as himself. A gramophone horn was connected to the record player and almost the size of the box itself. Tucked loosely underneath Circuit's arms was a collection of records.

"Circuit," Bog said, eyeing the records, "if you happen to

have Wagner's 'Ride of the Valkyries,' so help me, I'm going to give you your very own ship."

Circuit's eyes lit up, and he nearly dropped the record player. Setting the instrument in the center of the bridge he flipped through his records and pulled one free.

Bog's face pulled into a look of complete shock as the fluttering sound of violins blared through the gramophone followed by oboes and clarinets. "Circuit," he said, "you just earned yourself a dreadnought."

Jed

The dome was ablaze with war.

Jed thrashed at Lyle's ship.

Lyle's voice entered his head again. "You're acting like a child, Jed. Stop. You're only making this worse."

"I am a child," Jed yelled. He lifted an arm and punched a warnought's stern.

"You've forced my hand," Lyle said with a sigh. "I didn't want it to have to come to this, but you leave me no choice. Surrender, or your mother will die."

Jed's heart froze. The mower monster stumbled. "My mother?"

"Yes. Get out of that ridiculous pile of clunk, surrender yourself, and leave with me, or I will kill her. Am I clear?"

"You know where she is?"

"Of course I do." Lyle laughed. "She's been with us the whole time. Don't you remember?"

Something clicked in Jed's mind. How had he not noticed before? Despite the mechanical voice and the scraps of metal that had replaced her face, he knew the truth.

Alice.

Lyle read his thoughts. "It makes sense, doesn't it?" he taunted Jed. "You asked me why I couldn't fix her legs. Of course I can fix a clunky pair of legs. But why? She stole my future. In fact, her legs worked perfectly before I broke them. You know how delightful it is for me to watch her stumble around the *Endeavor*? It's delicious."

Jed's jaw clenched. "You're a monster," he whispered.

"We're all monsters," Lyle said. "Look at you!" He laughed. "You *literally* are a giant, shambling pile of lawn mowers. You're smashing dreadnoughts to bits. You're the biggest monster here."

Rage bubbled inside Jed. He yanked Lyle's vessels from the golden sky and crushed them, one by one.

"Stop this!" Lyle shouted. "You're going to kill everyone!"

"Let her go!" Jed shouted back. His voice was like a storm. "Now!"

"Jed," Lyle began, more softly. There was a hint of fear in his tone. "If you don't—"

Jed cut him off. "No more threats, Lyle," he said. "I am not your weapon. I will defend this city—and this world—for the rest of my life. And if you hurt my mom, you will regret ever putting a single spark into my body."

Silence.

"Where are you?" Jed shouted, trying to link to Lyle's mind once again.

"Good-bye, Jed," Lyle answered at last.

"Mom," Jed whispered, scanning the inside of the dome. "Where are you?"

If she were a machine, maybe he could speak with her through his mind. He closed his eyes and tried again.

"Mom," he said out loud. "Please be there."

A faint connection crackled.

"Mom, are you there?"

"Gzzz . . ."

The response was fuzzy and garbled.

"Mom," he said, "if you can understand this, send me a signal. Tell me where you are."

Jed scanned the dome. Explosions and rockets stained the skies, but a speck of light caught his attention, far away from the battle. It was a green battery bug fluttering in the distance. The battery bug from Trisky's Trinkets in Lunkway. The battery bug he'd given to Alice.

"I'm coming, Mom."

Jed

Jed kept his eyes locked on the light from the green battery bug and readied himself to hunt down the *Endeavor*. Just then, a whistle cut through the air.

Shay's voice crackled in his ear. "Umm ... there's more people here."

Jed recognized the whistling sound. Iron falcons.

A fleet of tiny shapes soared into the dome, firing at any dreadnought in their path. They didn't care if the ships belonged to Bog or Lyle. All they cared about was fighting the dread.

The dome was turning into chaos. Ships fluttered about like swarms of gnats. Both dreadnought armadas again swiveled to face this new enemy, dividing their focus and unleashing shatterfire at the swarming falcons. More followed, and more. Copper battlecruisers, mercenary freighters, and ruster junk ships joined next.

The metals had finally united against the dread.

But Jed couldn't stay and fight—he had a mom to rescue. Jed closed his eyes and drew in as much of the mountain's remaining battery power into his sparks as he could—more than he ever had before. "Time to go," he said to Sprocket.

Jed ripped the cable from his chest. Sparks dribbled from the loose wires and splashed around his feet. He flew to the window and leaped out into the open air. Wind rushed over him as he tumbled downward. Charging the ground with mutiny, he pushed hard against it. His body slowed until he hovered midway down the mountain. With a firm push, he then mutinied himself into the sky.

Jed flew through the air, rallying himself from ship to ship in deep, swooping motions.

"Alice," he shouted to Sprocket, who flew desperately after him. "We need to get Alice!"

He sailed toward the green battery bug, gliding through the air like a hawk. He spotted the *Endeavor* clinging to a corner of the dome like a spider in a web. Jed swiftly, quietly landed on top of a boxcar roof.

"I'm going to stop Lyle and rescue my mom," he whispered to Sprocket.

"Alllizzz," she hummed.

"But I need you to do something for me."

"Okaaay," Sprocket said cheerily. "Whaaat?"

"Figure out a way to stop all of that," Jed said, motioning to the thundering war behind them.

Sprocket turned in the air, her tin can face glancing at the burning warships and the whistling shatterfire. She glanced back to Jed. Then back to the war. And finally, back to Jed.

"Whattt?!"

Jed nodded once. "Yep. Just stop the war. That's it." He patted her head softly. "Good luck." Then he ripped open a train hatch and dropped inside.

Lyle stood before him, unsurprised, as if he'd been waiting for this. He was dressed in the mechanical suit from the spark cabin. Mutiny sparks clustered at the tip of its right arm.

"Hello, son," Lyle said with a smirk. "Come to watch the show with me?"

"It's over for you," Jed said. "You've lost."

Lyle smiled. "Look around," he said. "Everyone's lost. Not just me. Pretty soon, this world will be a graveyard. How many golds do you think will survive this battle? Have you ever seen a gold try to fight? They're pathetic. No matter who wins, all of *them* will die."

"What about your army?" Jed asked. "You're going to lose your fleet."

"Every corpse in this dome *will* be my army. The more that die, the better."

"You're insane."

Lyle shrugged. "Perhaps. But no more so than the fools out there trying to blow one another to scrap."

"Where is Alice?" Jed demanded.

Lyle reached into his pocket and retrieved the black key

he'd tried so many times to use on Jed. "Put this in your chest, and she's all yours."

"I'm not going to let you take control of every spark in my body," Jed said.

"I don't *just* need the sparks," Lyle said. "I need your frame, too. And I know you are too kind to let your meat sack mommy die." He held the key toward Jed.

Jed stared at the key. "And if I give you my power, you'll let my mom go?"

Lyle nodded slowly. "Yes."

Jed stepped forward and reached out his hand. Lyle's eyes glittered with anticipation.

But instead of taking the key, Jed clasped Lyle's hand.

The hunger in Lyle's face evaporated—replaced with apprehension. "What are you doing?" he asked.

Jed closed his eyes and released his power. "Giving you everything I have."

Lyle tried to pull away, but Jed rallied their palms together into an unbreakable grip. Lyle's gaze snapped to his. "Stop it."

Jed released more energy.

"Let go of me!" Lyle shouted. Lyle's arm glowed orange with heat. Jed felt bits of himself beginning to melt as well. Energy passed through their clasped hands. Lyle's face twisted into a scowl. His voice sealed as his features blurred and dripped into each other.

The last of Jed's energy dispersed. A biting cold washed through his blood. Blackness swirled through his vision and his knees buckled. He was a statue of ice, falling to the floor before a statue of molten gold.

Jed

"Jed!" a voice shouted. "Jed!"

A hand wrapped around his wrist. "Wake up, wake up!"

Jed opened his eyes. Shay's face hovered over him. Her nose was almost touching his. "Are you awake, Sleepy Mouse?"

Jed grumbled. His limbs were stiff and protested as he flexed them.

"What's going on?" he said. "How long was I out for?"

Shay's face scooted back, and she shrugged. "How should I know? I just got here and found you taking a nap. By the way, what in scritcher-snap-clunk is that thing?" She motioned to a figure standing before him.

"Lyle," Jed said.

Shay studied the mangled golden mess. "Is he still . . . ?"

"Alive?" Jed finished. Shay nodded. "I have no idea." He sat up. "Alice," he said to Shay. "Where is she?"

"Over here." Jed spun around. Alice sat in the corner of the train car. She gave him an uncomfortable wave. "Shay already told me," she said. "About the whole mom thing. It's just . . . I don't remember anything before waking up on the *Endeavor*. I'm sorry."

"You don't have to be sorry," Jed said. "I know exactly what that's like, not being able to remember anything. It feels like slug clunk."

She nodded, but the discomfort in her face remained.

"We'll figure it out," Jed said.

"How about you figure it out maybe after everyone stops killing each other?" Shay said, pointing out the window.

Jed stood and peered out at the battlefield. "We need to get them to stop fighting," he said. Explosions crackled throughout the dome as more and more ships clustered together, firing upon one another. "Lyle was right. This place is going to be a graveyard by morning."

He turned and gave Shay and Alice a helpless glance. "Anyone have any ideas?" he asked hopefully.

"What's that?" Shay asked, pointing to a violet light in the distance.

Jed turned and squinted at the light. It grew larger and larger until it looked to be the size of one the dreadnoughts. It hovered in the air, drifting closer to the cluster of warring ships.

An iron falcon broke away from the battle and launched

a series of rockets at the purple light. Just as the rockets drew near, the light burst into a million tiny dots. The falcon's rockets soared harmlessly past them and exploded into a patch of empty grass. The swarm of lights pulled back, paused, and then rushed toward the warring fleets.

"Battery bugs," Jed whispered. He turned and glanced at Alice. "They're battery bugs."

"Where'd they come from?" Shay asked.

Jed flashed back to when Sprocket danced with them around Lawnmower Mountain. Before he could answer, the purple battery bugs swarmed the ships still hammering one another with shatterfire.

One by one, the bugs winked out as they entered through cracks in the ships' hulls. Ugly grinding noises soon began to whine across the battlefield. Thick black smoke oozed from every engine and turbine that now struggled to function.

"She's actually doing it," Jed said.

"Who's doing what?" Shay asked.

"Sprocket," he said, grinning. "She's stopping the war."

Jed scrambled through the hatch and leaped from the *Endeavor*.

Battery bugs swarmed the remaining airborne vessels. They disappeared through vents, cracks, and exhaust valves. Wherever they entered, flurries of sparks showered from the sabotaged guts of the ships. Dreadnoughts, wasps, and falcons all writhed in the air.

A cloud of battery bugs danced in the center of it all.

They were a happy tornado of victory. Above them all, Sprocket fluttered unsteadily with her Ping-Pong paddle and Frisbee wings.

"Sprocket!" Jed shouted. "You did it!"

"Zzztop fight! Zzztop fight! Zzztop fight!"

Jed

Jed removed the sliver of spark from his mother's core and replaced it with an unbroken spark from his chest. As he infused it with energy, life surged through her. The metal fragments that made up her face softened as her single, violet eye met his.

"Jed," she whispered, sitting up and taking his face in her hands.

She pulled him into a gentle hug and he held her metal body. "I thought you were dead," he said in her ear.

"I was," she said. "But I'm back."

"You need to get out there," a voice said behind him.

Zix.

Jed looked out one of the *Endeavor*'s windows. Ships

littered the basin of the golden dome. Once green with grass, fields, and orchards, the land was now speckled with broken metal. Soldiers staggered from their vessels, unsure of what to do next.

"Can this thing still fly?" Jed asked.

"I'll spin up the ion battery," Zix said. "Dak, Brindle," he called down the corridor. The two dragonflies peeked out of one of the cabins. "Fix up the ship's loudspeaker system so the speakers point toward the outside of the ship."

"Aye, aye, boss," they called.

Zix handed Jed one of the microphones that Lyle had used to communicate with the crew. "I hope you have a good speech planned."

The *Endeavor* was in the air in seconds after Zix left the room. It flew to the center of the dome above a patch of lemon trees. Jed climbed through the top hatch and stood atop the train. The microphone's coiled cord barely reached. He squeezed the button of the microphone, and the loudspeaker amplified his voice, ringing out over the nearby ships.

"To every dread and dragonfly that can hear me: Lyle is gone. I have inside me the life he stole from you. But it's not mine to keep. Any of you that want to be what you once were, I can give that to you. I have enough sparks for every dread and dragonfly who wants one. Instead of the sliver of spark you have now, I will give each of you that wants one a full life spark. You can be everything you used to be before you died. Memories . . . life . . . personality."

A blast from a shatterbox held by a distant dread fired past him, nearly hitting his shoulder. "Get that clunker and scoop out all of the treasure inside him!" the dread shouted.

But before the dread could say another word, it burst into gears and scrap. Captain Bog holstered his shatterbox from afar and nodded to Jed.

Jed smiled at him. "Thanks."

He continued his speech, but none of the dread came forward. The more Jed spoke, the angrier they became. Eventually, Sprocket's battery bugs simply had to suppress their ships and weapons until Bog's ships could manage to police the area. Bog's forces guarded the dome as coppers and irons and dread repaired their vessels and departed.

Jed joined the others on the tugboat. "The irons and coppers know where the golds are now," Jed said to his dad, who stood with him on the main deck of the tugboat. "They'll probably come back like they did all those years ago."

Ryan nodded. "Probably. But the golds have something they never had before: They have you."

As the ships prepared to leave, only a few dread approached Jed about his offer. Most simply patched up their ships and left through the breach in the dome. Those who did ask for a spark seemed only to want a new "pretty treasure."

The gold city was in complete disarray. Scrap and carnage littered the once beautiful fields and orchards. Half of the pleasant cottages were now rubble. The golds themselves were rattled and didn't seem to know how to react to what had just happened to their home.

Jed called for Hift, Murjen, and Taskon. The three looked

like scared children as they emerged from their shelter and bumbled over to him.

"Do you know what I've been craving for as long as I can remember?"

Hift shook his head.

"A classic, New York–style pepperoni pizza and a huge pitcher of ice-cold lemonade. Have you ever had New York–style pizza?"

All three of them shook their heads.

Jed nodded. "I'll show you. Fire up the ovens. Let's make all of our guests here some pizza and lemonade before they leave."

Jed

A midst a hundred thousand tons of rubble, those still left in the dome after the coppers and irons and most of the dread were gone all gathered in the town square for pizza and lemonade. The gold cooks were exceptional. Before the first pepperoni pizza was even out of the oven, they were all discussing new toppings and configurations. Pretty soon, they had made: balsamic strawberry pizza, berry with arugula and prosciutto pizza, cantaloupe and sweet ricotta pizza, charred corn and avocado pizza, and a raspberry brie dessert pizza.

For a moment, it seemed everyone had forgotten about the terrible events of only just hours before. Golds laughed and chatted with Jed's family, the tugboat crew, and even attempted small talk with some of Bog's dread. Though . . . the dread didn't seem to know what to do with the pizza. They pinched it warily, sniffing it as though it were something highly suspicious.

Jed spotted Captain Bog and Shay talking with his parents and decided it was as good a time as any to tell them all what he had decided. With a deep breath, he walked over and smiled at the four. They smiled back. Well . . . Bog gave him a genial nod, at least . . . but that definitely counted as a smile in Jed's opinion.

"I've decided to stay," Jed said to his mom and dad. "This is my home. It's where I belong. And they're going to need me here now that the coppers and irons know where they live. Someday, they'll get greedy again and attack. If the golds couldn't defend themselves hundreds of years ago when they had a city of ten thousand golds, there's no way they'll make it now. They need me here."

His mom looked from his dad to Jed. "Then we'll stay, too," she said, taking his hand. "We're never leaving you again."

His dad nodded.

"And what about you?" Bog said, turning to Shay. "Does that mean you're staying here, too?"

Shay put her hands on her hips and stared straight into Captain Bog's face. "Have you ever had a perfectly cooked pomegranate pie? I have. Right here. And it's to die for. Melt-in-your-mouth delectable. Not to mention Shepin's kebabs . . ."

Bog nodded. "I guess . . . this is good-bye, then?"

"What do you mean?" Shay asked. "Of course I'm not

staying here. You think I'd give up flying around the world with the ickiest, scariest, meanest, biggest, rottenest, scoundreliest, scritchiest scritchmutt in all of Scritcherdom to stay here and get fat? Nuh-uh. Nope. No, no, no."

Bog's face lit up with a rare, wrinkled smile. "Then what was all that about the pomegranate pie and kebabs?" he asked.

"We need to make sure to get at least twenty pies before we leave," she said. "And whenever we come to visit, they better have a basketful of kebabs ready for us."

"Captain," Kizer said, approaching Bog with Riggs and Pobble. "Now that you're back, *Bessie*'s all yours. We'd be honored to have you as our captain again."

Bog shook his head. "She's all yours, Kizer. I've still got to figure out this mess I put myself in," he said, jutting his chin toward the fleet of dreadnoughts that hovered quietly in the corner of the dome. "You take care of her, you hear? She's a good ship." He rested an encouraging hand on Kizer's shoulder.

Kizer opened his mouth to speak, but before he could, Sprocket buzzed up beside him and floated right in front of his grim face. "Clllunnnk faaace," she said, buzzing even closer to Kizer. "Jed can clllimb a ladderrr. Up, up, uuup!"

"Huh?" Kizer said, looking to Jed.

Jed shrugged. "Apparently, not *everyone* thinks I'm useless at ladder climbing."

"So, you *did* know where a few other relics were . . ." Riggs said to Jed with a wink.

Jed looked around the dome and smiled. "Maybe a few, I guess."

"By the way," Pobble said, "forget about what I said before about not being able to call yourself 'big.' You know, what with you being a mountain and all."

. . .

By morning, the dome was empty once again. The invaders were gone, and all was quiet. Jed sat on a hilltop overlooking the gold village. In his hands he held the small brass key that had unlocked so much. The life sparks of an entire civilization pulsed inside him. He felt as if he'd strangely become their guardian. They were *his* people, and this was *his* home. No one would ever take that away from him again.

The skin on his chest had healed almost completely, leaving only the small keyhole. Jed lifted the old key to his chest and turned it the opposite direction—locking the new Jed he'd become. As a click sounded in the silence, he removed the key and set it into the hole he'd dug near his feet.

"Welcome home," he said to himself, filling the hole with dirt, and walking back toward the town.

Acknowledgments

I'd like to acknowledge some of those who helped make this a reality. First, to Mom: Thank you for always pushing me forward and for always believing in me. To Matthew: Thank you for the light of your friendship in the darkest of times. To Evan and Dillon: Your enthusiasm for *Jed* means more than you know. To Emma: Thank you again for the Tin Forest. It was perfect. And to Tracey, my tireless editor, and her whole editorial staff: You all are truly incredible mouselings.